THE DARK SIDE OF THE PYRAMID

Special Bonus Section:
The complete text of
Fake It Till You Make It
by Philip Kerns

As seen on *60 Minutes* and the
Phil Donahue Show

Patrick J. Smith, MBA
Copyright © 2002-2003 All rights reserved

XULON PRESS

The Dark Side of the Pyramid
by Patrick J. Smith

Printed in the United States of America

Library of Congress Control Number: 2003092688
ISBN 1-591606-72-1

Xulon Press
www.XulonPress.com

Xulon Press books are available in bookstores everywhere,
and on the Web at www.XulonPress.com.

Table of Contents

Introduction

My wife asked me why I wanted to write this book. When I was young I believed the best about people and I just knew that there was still the right "opportunity" waiting for me just around the corner. I used to have a positive outlook on life. It didn't used to be part of my nature to go on the attack and cut through all of the smoke and mirrors. In a way, that is what made me an easy target for those involved in network marketing when I first was starting out in my professional career. The reason that I'm writing this book is summed up by Ecclesiastes 3. It says:

> *"There is a time for everything, and a season*
> *for every activity under heaven:*
>   *...a time to plant and a time to uproot,*
>   *a time to tear down and a time to build,*
>   *a time to be silent and a time to speak..."*

Also, 1 Corinthians 13:11 reminds us that:

> *"When I was a child, I talked like a child, I*
> *thought like a child, I reasoned like a child. When*
> *I became a man, I put childish ways behind me."*

This book was originally intended as a follow-up to Philip Kerns' book, *Fake It Till You Make It,* which was published in December of 1982. Kerns' focus was on a single network marketing company by the name of Amway. This book is not targeted at any specific company, although many of the examples in the book are drawn primarily from my experiences with Amway during a fifteen year time span. The principles outlined in this book are targeted against the all of the shady sponsors that still permeate the entire network marketing industry, not just Amway.

Two full decades will have passed by the time this book goes to press. The network marketing companies have had more than enough time to clean up the mess that has been created by their overenthusiastic star performers. The Millennium may have changed, but sadly the tactics used by people within the industry have not. I have watched with wonder and dismay as the techniques become more and more blatant and shrewd.

Over the past few years I have been approached by friends who have gotten caught up in network marketing schemes, and they have asked me to evaluate a number of "opportunities." Time after time I have been able to pinpoint to within weeks of when a network marketing company will stop paying bonus checks and "crash and burn" or go out of business. It is apparent that there is a general lack of understanding in the marketplace about network marketing (multi-level marketing, MLM, networking, matrix marketing, etc.). The information contained in this book could potentially save you hundreds or even thousands of dollars. Five value-packed sections are included in this book:

- **Part One** gives you access to over twenty-five years of network marketing experience and it exposes the thirty dark secrets that the person trying to sponsor you hopes that you never find out.

- **Part Two** is an evaluation guide that will help you evaluate the company, the network, and yourself in case you actually decide to pursue a career in network marketing. Perhaps you won't need this section after reading the other sections of this book. But, if you still need to use this section, you'll be tapping over twenty-five years of network marketing experience with the inside knowledge that you need to ask the right questions.

- **Part Three** is a humorous look at an imaginary network marketing company named Façade Line International and is a spoof on the network marketing industry. This will make you smile—unless, of course, you take networking much too seriously. A special note of thanks is due to my friend Bill because without his input this section would not have been possible. His ability to see the irony and humor in situations that network marketers take so seriously is worth its weight in gold.

- **Part Four** is a listing of Internet links: company and distributor sites, sites your sponsor hopes that you never see, and newsgroups (Usenet). This part was developed by an Internet search professional and is divided into two main sections. A novice surfer could easily save thirty or more hours of online and research time. An expert surfer could expect to save between five to ten hours of time with just this section alone:

  – The first section provides you internet links for many of the network marketing companies that are still in existence today.

- The second section is the "graveyard" of network marketing sites and companies that existed eight years ago when the list was compiled the first time but are no longer "on the net" or in the network marketing or MLM business.
- The sections in Part IV were originally one long list eight years ago when the research on the websites were first conducted. The list was twenty-six pages long in the standard 8.5-by-11-inch format. Now the graveyard is now over nineteen pages long, and the "survivors" from the original list is just over six pages long. This means that almost seventy-five percent of network companies on this list failed in the first eight years or less. That isn't really so remarkable as compared to other industries where the mortality rates are pretty much the same. Starting any new business is a risk, and most companies do not survive even the first five years for a number of reasons. Still, for every company that has closed its doors, another one has popped up to replace it.

- **Part Five** is a special bonus section especially for my readers—this is the complete text of the original book by Philip Kerns, *Fake It Till You Make It*. This section was included only at the last minute before this book went to press. The author of this book has not even had the opportunity to read the original yet, but his research team has informed him that the parallels between the two are eerie, even though the manuscripts were independently written twenty years apart.

This book is an absolute "must-have" for anyone who is serious about network marketing. It doesn't matter if you are pro-network marketing or anti-network marketing; this book is for you:

- If you are currently involved with *any* network marketing company, then you'll want to buy this book as a reference guide to learn how to withstand some of the most difficult questions ever posed to the network marketing industry. Or, maybe you'll just want to buy a copy and burn it to take one more copy out of circulation.

- If you dislike network marketing, then this book is your ultimate self-defense! Keep a copy handy and use it on the next network marketing person who tries to recruit you into his latest "opportunity." Hopefully this book will help those of you who still insist in pursuing a network marketing career to at least have a tool with which to assess the company you are considering joining.

Just for the record, my wife and I achieved the "Silver" level in Amway in the late 1980's, and we still have the pins in a box to prove it. Before you go rushing off to check corporate records there at Amway, please be aware that Patrick J. Smith is not my real name. For the safety of my friends and family, all names and events in this book have been altered to protect everyone's privacy. Other network marketing companies with which I have also been involved during the past include Enrich, Nikken, and countless others that I've already forgotten.

It has been a true "like/dislike" relationship between me and network marketing since the first time I was introduced to the "plan" as a young adult. A friend of mine came home from college for a short visit and said, "You should sign up as an Amway distributor, you're perfect for this business!" I didn't know what "Amway" was so I asked, "Sign up for what?" I was about to find out.

The Dark Side of the Pyramid rips the façade off the entire network marketing industry and exposes the cold, harsh reality of the sinister side of these questionable programs.

Patrick J. Smith, MBA

Legal Disclaimer: During the past twenty-five years, the author has participated in thousands of hours and taken innumerable pages of notes from many speakers, from many great trainers, and from many people involved in the network marketing industry. Having personally participated in a number of network marketing plans and having either personally experienced or watched first hand these plans and techniques in action, due to the time spans involved, it is possible that the many of the quotes in each chapter at first glance may appear to be similar to other authors' works on this subject. My goal is to be completely fair with everyone. To the best of my knowledge and ability, I have attributed the quotes, where possible, to their original authors. All other quotes in this book are the intellectual property of (and from) the author and other contributors to this project. All Bible passages quoted in this book are from the New International Version (NIV) (© Copyright 1973, 1978, 1984 by the International Bible Society. All rights reserved worldwide). All trade names, trademarks, service marks, etc. mentioned in this book are the sole property of their owners and their respective companies.

PART I

THE THIRTY DARK SECRETS

Chapter 1

Censorship

Secret 1. Intimidation—Philip Who?

"Silence isn't always golden."

If you can't defeat the truth, then bury it in litigation, threaten it, pay it off, or intimidate if necessary. Network marketing companies will do whatever is necessary to control the damage that the truth can do. One example is Philip Kerns, who authored and self-published the book *Fake It Till You Make It* in December of 1982. It is truly amazing that although over one million copies were allegedly sold, it is next to impossible to obtain a copy of this book anywhere. I'm still looking for an original copy in hardcover or paperback (I've been told that it has been out of print for around fifteen years).

I have friends who claim to have had seen or even held a copy in their hands, but I'm still waiting to even see even just one original copy. I once saw a used copy for sale on Amazon.com, but it was gone before I could bid on it. Rumor has it that orders came down "from the top" that "every copy was to be purchased and burned" by the distribution network. They seem to have succeeded in completing that task very, very well.

There have been many cases where the big and powerful networking companies have gone to court to ask for restraining orders against former employees and/or distributors from writing "tell-all" books. What are the deep, dark secrets of the pyramid that these companies want to keep from the general public? When you've got something to hide and are willing to go to those lengths to "protect" yourself, then you end up looking as guilty as charged. By the way, I wonder whatever did happen to Philip Kerns.

Amway successfully quieted the voice of Philip Kerns and dozens of others who have been willing to stand up and speak the truth. There are probably more than thirty dark secrets, and I'm sure that others may have uncovered fifty, seventy-five, or even hundreds of secrets during their lifetimes. Because of the size and political strength of the network marketing industry, they have the power to quash any voices that paint them in a negative light.

The network marketing companies are convinced that their "systems" are good. But are they really "good?" The other twenty-nine dark secrets that are revealed in this book will cause you to stop and ponder just how "good" the network marketing companies really are.

> *Psalm 38:20: "Those who repay my good with evil slander me when I pursue what is good."*
>
> *Psalm 101:8: "Every morning I will put to silence all the wicked in the land; I will cut off every evildoer from the city of the LORD."*
>
> *Isaiah 5:20: "Woe to those who call evil good and good evil, who put darkness for light and*

light for darkness, who put bitter for sweet and sweet for bitter."

Secret 2. Free Speech is Not Free Enterprise

"Give me network marketing or give me death!"

V ivid memories flash before my eyes as I remember my sponsor's response when I asked him specifically about Kerns' book. He went into a mode I had never seen before. It was almost chilling. He became really agitated, but tried to cover it up by being way too "sugary sweet" and nice to me. He then asked to see a copy of the book. I asked why he was so interested in that book, but he never really answered why. Immediately my "radar" went off, and I knew that I had hit a raw nerve. Anything that he wanted that badly had to be good. I'm quite certain that had I been able to get a copy and share it with him that he would have made sure that it disappeared, never to see the light of day again.

Is it a "good offense is the best defense" or a "good defense is a best offense?" Either way, the book wars continue. The network marketing companies will go to great lengths defensively to keep detractors from publishing their experiences. On the other hand, they're more than happy to use the same tactics as the detractors when they want to spin network marketing in a positive light. Just the other day when I was in the local bookstore, I noticed that someone had written another favorable book on the subject of network marketing. It was part defense, part propaganda, and part "how-to." The book itself was a rather pathetic attempt to counteract all of the "bad" publicity that the network marketing industry has received during the past couple of decades. I'm not going to waste your time by refuting that book point by point because this book contains probably everything that you will ever need to refute and counter any of the claims made in that, or any other, "pro" network marketing book.

It's important to remember that each and every network marketing sponsor's worst nightmare is the person who is armed with the right questions. Feel free to ask the right questions at the next meeting you attend, but be prepared to suffer the wrath of the group. Free speech and free enterprise don't necessarily share the same space, especially if in the name of free speech a "free enterprise" is identified as a scam. Typically what will happen is that a person who has been burned by a network marketing company will become angry enough to contact the local media outlets to prevent others from suffering the same fate that he did. The local media is always hot for the latest scandal and usually publishes whatever the wronged distributor or customer wants to tell.

However, the damage control teams that the network marketing companies employ are truly impressive. First, they trot out their association with the Pope (yes, one company has had the guts to be so bold), royalty of various countries, or other ties to the government or even to the UN! Next, they hire a battery of lawyers and judges from the country or state in question who then declare the program "legal." Most network companies anticipate the types of problems that they'll encounter in advance and have already done the legal "groundwork" to have their system approved by the local government. Finally, when the media attacks begin, they counterattack with their lawyers and with the "fact" that they've already been "legally" cleared for business in that region.

It's interesting that their strategy is to have the program declared "legal." Nobody seems to ever question whether or not it's ethical or moral. Are these network marketing programs legal? Since the sponsors will insist that theirs is a "people" business and NOT a "product" business, then most companies today really aren't legal anymore. In all of the network marketing programs in which I've participated, there was always the pressure the build volume, so products were rarely, if ever, sold at the listed retail price. Are the programs really moral? You will have to be the judge of that. From my perspective, any company that needs to parade an association with the Pope, members of royal families, etc. is already suspect.

Psalm 31:18: "Let their lying lips be silenced, for with pride and contempt they speak arrogantly against the righteous."

Proverbs 16:13: "Kings take pleasure in honest lips; they value a man who speaks the truth."

Chapter 2

Smoke and Mirrors

Secret 3. Illusion

"Is that Rolex real?"

W ho doesn't want to be successful? The lure of the bright lights, fame and fortune never ceases to attract millions every year, like moths drawn to the flame, into network marketing "plans." It starts out so simple. First, you're invited by a friend that you haven't seen since high school to a meeting to examine some kind of "business opportunity" or, if they're really sneaky, they'll just want to go out for a "cup of coffee."

When you show up to meet for coffee, you immediately realize something is not right. You can feel it. Your friend really wasn't interested in coffee, and he or she had a hidden motive for inviting you out. Or, when you arrive at the conference center for the Friday evening meeting in blue jeans and casual shirt, everywhere you look are nothing but blue suits, crisp white shirts, and red power ties, and you realize that you don't fit in. All of the expensive, upscale cars and SUV's in the parking lot should have tipped you off as you drove into the conference center's parking lot. Everyone you meet seems to be wearing a gold Rolex, gold tie chain, and gold cufflinks with diamonds, and is carrying an oversized day planner heavy enough to break your foot. The dance around the golden calf is about to begin, and it's too late to escape.

As the meeting begins with energetic, pulsating, driving rock music, a persuasive leader takes the stage and the crowd erupts in a wild frenzy of adoration. Welcome to your first network marketing meeting. It's like a rock concert, revival meeting, and motivational sales pitch all rolled into one giant, juicy business burrito. Slather on a little enchanting salsa and there is no denying the enthusiasm, energy, or seduction of the meeting. Somebody is definitely happy and excited about something here, but from everything I seen and heard, there is nothing behind the act that I'm seeing onstage. It's all a façade that is cleverly designed to deceive people into departing with their hard-earned cash and free time.

As I begin to ask questions, people stare at me in disbelief. "Who is this pagan?" "Who let a 'non-believer' through the door?" "Infidel!" You would have thought I had passed gas in church or something like that by simply asking questions. "Don't question; just believe," I was told. Well, I soon learned that if they can't dazzle you with their brilliance, then they'll try to baffle you with their "smoke and mirrors." What makes someone believe that they will succeed when the odds are truly against them? Eventually I learned the hard way the cold, hard truths that are contained in this book.

Illusion is one of their basic tools. You will hear things like:

- "To be successful, you have to look successful. It's ALL an act. Look the part, exude enthusiasm, and buy whatever props you need to become what you want to be. I did it, and you can, too!"

- "You need to buy at one level above where you are right now to create an aura of credibility. It doesn't matter what is real; it matters only what you want reality to be."

- "Do you want to be a millionaire? Then start dressing, talking, and traveling like one. Buy the right luxury car. Nobody is going to believe you if you show up in a ten-year-old wreck."

I've observed a number of people during the last twenty-five years who have ended up becoming what I call "network marketing casualties." Everyone has a friend or two like "Gary," "Ned," and "Fred." Maybe you'll recognize them. Maybe you won't. And, if you've never met anyone like them, you will in this book. Names have been changed to protect the "guilty," and they are each worthy of a book all by themselves. I have never seen so many spectacular near successes in the world of free enterprise as I have with this team of winners. Yet, in spite of all this, each time a new "opportunity" comes along, they are ready to dive in head-first without first looking to see how deep the pool is before they dive. Splat!

The sponsors have to create an illusion of success to reach an organizational critical mass for their group of distributors (also known as a "downline") where a "breakthrough" occurs and the process becomes self-replicating. Duplicating your own effort is crucial if you are going to build a successful network marketing organization and leverage your investment of time and money. A duality is at work here. The very "hype" and illusion that help a company to reach critical mass in the beginning are the very things that sow the seeds of failure for the network companies in the end. Promises are made by the sponsor and expectations for the new recruit are set that are basically unrealistic and unachievable. The network marketing industry has had to pay out millions of dollars in damages to former distributors that have sued them and won.

Most people do not have the discipline required to drive their own enterprise and should probably be working for someone else. Unfortunately, the perfect "test" that can identify who will succeed and who will fail in trying to "build" this kind of business doesn't exist yet. Some of the most unlikely candidates will become superstars, while those that seem as though they should succeed end up going down in flames and fail miserably.

It also appears that the network marketing industry is not alone because to some extent every company seems to "fake it till they make it" in the beginning. It doesn't matter what the industry or product is—a certain amount of pretending goes on until the company reaches critical mass and can survive. The playacting and deception has become so rampant in the software industry, for example, that a new term has been coined for it: "vaporware." The goal of this book is to help you cut through the haze spewed out by the legions of network marketing sponsors who are trying to worm their way into your life and wallet. When you are finished with this book, you will be able to distinguish a "vapornet" from a legitimate opportunity.

Proverbs 13:7: "One man pretends to be rich, yet has nothing; another pretends to be poor, yet has great wealth."

Ecclesiastes 9:11: "I have seen something else under the sun: The race is not to the swift or the battle to the strong, nor does food come to the wise or wealth to the brilliant or favor to the learned; but time and chance happen to them all."

Secret 4. Delusion

"I believe; therefore, I am a distributor."

One time my friend Gary decided to become a distributor for a pepper-spray personal security product line. Gary wanted to make sure that the product was as safe and effective as advertised. He sprayed a short burst of the chemical onto his hands and applied it like after-shave on his neck to test it on himself. Fifteen minutes later, when his eyes had stopped watering like a fire hose, he was finally able to drag himself up off the floor. He had just confirmed, firsthand, just how effective this product was. Guess who he called next? That's right, me! "Hey, Patrick, have I got an opportunity for you!" This is just what I needed, another "opportunity."

Each new networking program or "opportunity" that comes along reminds me of the pepper spray. There is always the hope that maybe this time around things will be different. But just like the pepper spray, you usually end up on the floor writhing in agony as your pocketbook is slowly and methodically drained of cash. The effects eventually wear off over time, and the results are usually the same. You pick yourself off the floor, dust yourself off, and immediately start looking for the next great opportunity again!

It reminds me of the song, "Have you heard about the

lonesome loser? He's a loser but he still keeps on trying...."
It takes a certain amount of self-delusion to be able to keep
a positive, "free-enterprise" attitude after multiple experiences like the pepper spray.

There are all kinds of mental gymnastics that someone
needs to go through to succeed in this business. First and
most important, if you really want to succeed in network
marketing, then you have to be able to put all of your ethics
and morals in the closet and take them out and brush them
off for "show and tell" only on Sunday.

> *2 Thessalonians 2:11: "For this reason God
> sends them a powerful delusion so that they will
> believe the lie."*

Secret 5. The Big One

"Really, this one is going to be huge!"

If I had a dollar for every time that I've heard the line,
"This program is going to go like a rocket," I would have
a nice down payment on a very big house by now. What else
is a sponsor supposed to say—"This program is really a pile
of horse manure, and we'll be lucky if you even sign up"? It
never ceases to amaze me that every new program that I've
seen in the last two decades is "the big one." "This one's different because (enter whatever the reason is on this line):
_____."

The lure here is really, really good. It is the only thing
that can explain why three hundred of my neighbors in my
community plunked down over $300,000 (U.S.) on a "gold"
coin network marketing scam. That's right—they each
plopped down over one thousand dollars in the hopes of

earning four hundred dollars per month on a product that is purchased only once by each distributor. Sadly, most of the people who have left that program have admitted that they were sucked in by their own desire for making more money.

It's easy to understand them because who wouldn't have wanted to be in on the ground floor of purchasing stock in Coca-Cola, IBM, Microsoft, Nokia, Levi Strauss, etc.? But why is it that every new network marketing company that hits the market claims to be the next IBM or Microsoft? It's true that your chances for success are better if you're in from the beginning, but most new network marketing companies go bust or just simply disappear as you will see in the "graveyard" in Part IV of this book.

The reason that most new network marketing companies go bankrupt is that they never reach the level of critical mass or market credibility that's necessary for them to withstand losing fifty percent of all of their distributors each and every year. Companies that survive long enough to achieve critical mass will end up making their owners incredibly wealthy. The people at the top of the pyramid won't do too badly, either.

It's the poor guy at the bottom of the pyramid who is shouldering the weight of the entire organization. His investment in himself and his dream is enabling a lifestyle for the chosen few that most of us can only read or dream about.

Proverbs 19:21: "Many are the plans in a man's heart, but it is the LORD's purpose that prevails."

Ecclesiastes 4:4: "And I saw that all labor and all achievement spring from man's envy of his neighbor. This too is meaningless, a chasing after the wind."

Chapter 3

Emotional Manipulation

Secret 6. Dream Thieves

*"Just when you thought it was
safe to share your dreams."*

I nvest in your dream," they keep telling you. OK. But what
happens when my dream doesn't match your dream?
What happens when my recruit's dreams don't match mine?
How do you get someone to invest in any dream, let alone
yours? The following series of questions and follow-ups are
one of the classic network marketing emotional manipulation techniques.

The first question that a sponsor asks his prospect is,
"What would you do with an extra $100,000?" The
"prospect" writes down what he would do with the extra
cash. This is invaluable information for the sponsor. This
question just identified the prospect's "needs."

The follow-up question is even more powerful: "What

would you do with an extra $10,000,000?" You have to think big here. The prospect then writes down what he'd do with the extra cash (the items listed on this list have to be different from the original list). This question just identified the prospect's "dreams."

The sponsor is now equipped with the necessary information with which to manipulate or motivate the prospect, depending upon your point of view. Even more remarkable is that the prospect volunteered the information freely.

Another twist on this technique is to substitute "time" for money, that is, "What would you do with another twenty hours per week?" Either way, they've got you. If you really want to drive a person who's trying to sponsor you nuts, then just tell him that you wouldn't change a thing with your time or money—that you're content and happy where you are, even if you aren't. Then sit back and watch him come apart at the seams. This is live entertainment at its best.

The question that needs to be asked here is "What happens when the person fails?" Most of the time the sponsor will blame the person—"You didn't dream big enough." Or, "You didn't follow my instructions 'exactly.'"

What really happens when the new distributor fails? First, he stops being active. Then he stops buying the products altogether. And finally, he eventually ends up leaving the business for good (the rate of distributors quitting each year in most network marketing companies exceeds fifty percent), and his dreams have been stolen and used against him for someone else's short-term gain. Any legitimate sponsor will work very hard to keep this from happening. The ill will that this builds for the sponsor's network marketing company is huge. Every person who walks away with bad feelings toward the sponsor and the network marketing company will negatively influence at least the 200+ people who are in his circle of influence.

Let's put that into some perspective. One network marketing company that has been in business for over forty years currently has a couple of million of distributors in the U.S. A turnover rate of fifty percent per year means that at least twenty million people have at one time or another been involved with that particular program during the past forty years! If only half of those people had a really negative experience, that means that they would have a negative impact on over 200 million of their friends and family. That doesn't leave much of a market left when you consider that there are only around 270 million men, women, and children in the U.S.

In people's minds, the battle has already been lost. The small percentage of mind-share allocated in people's minds has already been tainted by, "Oh yeah, friend Gary tried that once. He spent thousands of dollars on tapes, rallies, and seminars and still never even broke even." "He always was a dreamer." That's the cold, hard reality that sooner or later every distributor and network company must face.

Your dreams are yours and yours alone. Guard them with your life. Never share your dreams with a friend, relative, or stranger, especially if you know that he is a network marketer.

Psalm 73:20: "As a dream when one awakes, so when you arise, O Lord, you will despise them as fantasies."

Ecclesiastes 5:3: "As a dream comes when there are many cares, so the speech of a fool when there are many words."

Ecclesiastes 5:7: "Much dreaming and many words are meaningless. Therefore stand in awe of God."

Secret 7. Perspective Is Reality

"Dream, dream, dream, la, la, la, la, la..."

Using a new distributor's dreams to manipulate his perspective with his permission is a standard network marketing technique. What is happening here is subtle, yet vital for success (your sponsor's success, not yours). Once the sponsor knows a new distributor's needs and dreams, using those to "motivate" (manipulate) him into action becomes an easy task. Words are chosen very carefully. Enthusiasm and excitement builds and the new distributor ends up highly motivated by his own greed, needs, and dreams, and ends up buying into the program! The next step is to reshape the new recruit's perspective.

Manipulating people's perspective is easy because what most people fail to realize is that over time, most individuals will earn in excess of one million dollars within their lifetime anyway. If a family has an average income of thirty-five thousand dollars per year and works for thirty years, then they will have earned over one million dollars! With proper financial management, anyone can retire well on even only a modest income. If you're depending upon the government to provide your retirement income when you're old, then you're in for a big, bad surprise at the end of the road. Since most people don't look at the long-term perspective, then short-term gains can be really enticing.

The brainwashing and repositioning of the new prospect's perspective has only just begun at this point in time. At one weekend seminar that I attended, my upline sponsor made the following statements:

- "The *way* you think (not intelligence) determines success; your attitude is everything."
    - While that statement is probably true, it's the motivation behind it that needs to be questioned. I've seen many people succeed that weren't necessarily the brightest in the class, but they had the right attitude in spite of not being so smart. They were also like pit bulls with a wet bone and persevered where most everyone else would have turned tail and run.

- "Every career has "tools" and so does ours—TRUTH does not require your acceptance."
    - Hello! Did you catch that last line? Truth does not require your acceptance. It's sad that this is also probably true, and even sadder that it requires so much of your wallet!

Put your brains on hold, people! Check them at the door with your coat. Just believe, man, believe. Remember, the chief aim of marketing is to confuse the customer enough (a.k.a. "differentiation") so that the customer buys your product or service instead of your competitor's. Network marketers are experts in supplying confusion and well-crafted half-truths. And if you can't confuse them, then baffle, shame, or ridicule them—whatever works.

> *Proverbs 12:9: "Better to be a nobody and yet have a servant than pretend to be somebody and have no food."*

Secret 8. Network Junkies and Gullible George

"There really is one born every minute..."

L et the buyer beware. Secrets 8 through 10 bring us to the opportunity seeker (network flavor-of-the-month). These poor souls can be classified as seekers of the network "holy grail" or "ground floor" junkies. The ground floor is the first level of distributors that are directly sponsored by a network marketing company. There is this huge misconception that just because you're in on the ground floor you'll somehow make it to the top of this new organization. Network junkies are always seeking the next ground floor "quick fix," but never quite find it.

Everyone knows a "Gullible George." I have two friends named Fred and Ned *(again, their names have been changed to protect the innocent or the gullible guilty in this case)*. I have watched in amazement as, time after time, these two gentlemen have created network organizations with four hundred to six hundred distributors in each of their "downlines." A "downline" consists of the groups of distributors in the sponsor's entire organization. This doesn't even count the thousands of customers that each of their networks served. The most amazing thing is that they have barely made enough income to survive. I'm not convinced that they have ever done better financially than break-even.

The average combined total purchasing power of four hundred people may be as high as seven million dollars per year or more. And yet, Fred and Ned have never made more than fifteen hundred dollars per month (less than three-tenths of one percent of the total purchasing power of the group). But they'll be the first to be in on the "ground floor" of the next great opportunity. What am I missing here? I don't get it.

Although Fred and Ned have understood the "networking" part of the equation, they have never seemed to grasp the idea of building customers for life. The cost of customer acquisition in this business is just outrageous. Depending upon your business, acquiring a customer can cost anywhere from a couple of hundred dollars to several thousands of dollars per customer. For example, if it costs only two hundred dollars per customer, then four hundred people signed up as distributors (wholesale customers) represent an investment of eighty thousand dollars in acquisition costs alone!!! If I'm earning only fifteen hundred dollars per month, then to recover my cost of acquisition would take over fifty-three months! That's almost four and a half years!

To put this in the broader perspective, using just the two hundred dollar acquisition cost, that means that the company mentioned earlier that has lost over twenty million distributors (customers) during the last 40 years has had a customer acquisition cost of over $4.1 billion (yes, billion!). Well, actually it wasn't the company that shouldered this cost; it was the distributor organization that footed the bill on this one. It's interesting to note that the founding families' net wealth has been estimated at somewhere between four and five billion dollars. Is it possible that there be some kind of relationship between these two things? It should cause one to stop and think.

Each and every time Fred and Ned build a new network and it crashes, they destroy their credibility with that network of people. When the next "big one" comes around, they have to start from scratch again. Maybe that's why they're only scratching out a living. No business can survive long-term if it has to continually find new customers to replace the old ones.

Some savvy network marketers have created an income stream from using a "start-ups only" strategy. They have identified a network of Gullible Georges who will jump on the bandwagon each and every time they come up with the latest and greatest scheme. People like Fred and Ned are a sponsor's dream. Not only are they confused, but they also haven't understood that they'll never make it. Unfortunately, there is a ready supply of Gullible Georges out in the marketplace who are more than happy to part with their hard-earned money for a shot at the "big one." Just around the corner is the "Big Opportunity." How sad.

A number of resources are on the Internet and in communities to help people with this type of addiction. In some cases with some companies it might be necessary to retain the services of a professional cult deprogrammer.

> *Romans 16:18: "For such people are not serving our Lord Christ, but their own appetites. By smooth talk and flattery they deceive the minds of naive people."*

Secret 9. Trust

"Never trust a smiling blue suit."

T rust me." The delivery is so smooth, so warm, so fuzzy, so friendly and so sweet. The sad thing is that, for the most part, these people really are genuine, especially the poor saps in the trenches. People want to believe that they can trust others to tell the truth and will spread misinformation unintentionally.

If the chief aim of marketing is to "mix up" the customer (a.k.a. "differentiation"), then the chief aim of sales is to manipulate the perplexed customer into action resulting in the sale of your product or service. People will buy from you if they trust you. In the long term, the credibility of the networking industry suffers every time a sponsor breaks this trust.

Integrity is such a rare commodity in the business world today that how can the public trust anything anyone says about any "opportunity" anymore? It's like a variation of the old political joke: "How do you know when a network marketer is lying? That's right, his or her lips are moving." The economic harm that can occur due to misplaced trust is huge. Don't be taken in by sweet words delivered by sincere salespeople. The one thing that network companies can bank on is that people in general seem to want to be deceived. They seem to want someone to take advantage of them. Like the alcoholic or the gambling addict, they tell themselves, "It's just this one more time." They con themselves and say something like, "I can quit any time I want." Network junkies are always in search of another fix.

They have to trust the one who says, "This one is going to go like a rocket, too." There's no other explanation for their bizarre behavior. What they keep forgetting is that rockets fly only so far, and if they don't gain a high enough altitude to achieve orbit, they crash. Attitude does not determine altitude, and it cannot overcome the effects of a trust that has been broken.

Proverbs 3:5–6: "Trust in the LORD with all your heart and lean not on your own understanding; in all your ways acknowledge him, and he will make your paths straight [or, 'he will direct your paths']."

Secret 10. Belief

"Yeah, right!"

Y ou have to have the right belief and establish the right posture, and the performance of your network will take care of itself." As with any philosophy of life, to succeed, one must choose what one believes. Your sponsor wants you to empty yourself. To "deprogram" you of all of those years of negative influences from your family, friends, coworkers, schools, churches, and so on, you must become like a dry sponge in the desert of life, ready to soak up whatever the sponsor decides to rain down on you.

All of the manipulation techniques described in this book are a subtle art that is passed on from Sponsor to Distributor. No thinking is required. "Just believe, obey orders, and you'll succeed." "If you allow your 'old' beliefs to influence your thinking, then you won't succeed." Changing the prospect's belief system is the key to changing their attitudes and, ultimately, their behavior. If you want to change a person's actions then you'll need to reprogram their belief system.

A particularly disturbing trend in network marketing integrates people's political and/or religious views into a network marketing program to create a façade of political or religious acceptability. You wouldn't believe how many times I've been told, "The people behind this company are 'Republicans,' 'Democrats,' 'Independents,' 'Christians;' 'Muslims,' 'Hindus,' Buddhists, 'New Agers,' 'Humanists,' or whatever (enter your favorite "ism" here: _____), so you can trust them." Oh really?

Any time anyone needs to use a person's politics or religion as a way to build credibility for his or her program— RUN! I have been hurt more times by people of my own political party or faith than by all the "heathens" or "pagans" in the world combined. Please stop using God to promote your network. Oh, you say that you give gifts to your church, synagogue, mosque, etc.? Good. Just remember: God doesn't need your money to get His work done.

> *2 Timothy 3:2–7: "People will be lovers of themselves, lovers of money, boastful, proud, abusive, disobedient to their parents, ungrateful, unholy, without love, unforgiving, slanderous, without self-control, brutal, not lovers of the good, treacherous, rash, conceited, lovers of pleasure rather than lovers of God—having a form of godliness but denying its power. Have nothing to do with them. They are the kind who worm their way into homes and gain control over weak-willed women, who are loaded down with sins and are swayed by all kinds of evil desires, always learning but never able to acknowledge the truth."*

Secret 11. Free Enterprise, the Cult

> *"Come along, sing our song;*
> *sing our song of group 'think-ola…'"*

Stars and stripes forever, baseball, mom, and apple pie in the sky. It seems that many people have a deep yearning to be part of something "bigger than yourself." People seem to be so starved socially that, like a person who's drowning, they'll grab on to the first person who pays any attention to them, regardless of the short- or long-term costs.

Other books are devoted entirely to the subject of cults and how network marketing companies employ the same techniques and tools as the cults do. Free Enterprise has become a new type of cult in America. I have heard countless numbers of times sincere people make statements such as, "I belong. I believe. I trust my sponsor and the company completely."

Patriotism, faith in God, country, and family are all tools used by the skilled sponsor to manipulate the faithful. It's truly amazing what is being sold and what is being bought. Instead of getting suckered in, you should probably just walk away. It's sad that someone would use your beliefs to manipulate you into something that in the long run will not benefit you.

I remember one couple saying at a rally how wonderful it was that they could work together, and that the "business" had brought them "closer" together. I guess the closeness generated by working together wasn't a good thing in this case because they got divorced a couple of years later. If you're having trouble in your marriage, do yourself a favor and try counseling instead of network marketing. Counseling will probably cost less in the long run, too.

I've attended more than one weekend seminar that has made me more than uncomfortable. The whole format was like an old-fashioned tent revival, but the message shared at the meeting had nothing to do with the message that Jesus taught. They have the façade of being religious, but I doubt that Jesus would ever sign up for any network marketing program.

> *Jeremiah 14:14: "Then the LORD said to me, 'The prophets are prophesying lies in my name. I have not sent them or appointed them or spoken to them. They are prophesying to you false visions, divinations [or visions, worthless divinations], idolatries and the delusions of their own minds.'"*

Galatians 1:8: "But even if we or an angel from heaven should preach a gospel other than the one we preached to you, let him be eternally condemned!"

2 Timothy 3:5: "...having a form of godliness but denying its power. Have nothing to do with them."

Secret 12. Divide, Conquer and Alienate

"Network marketers are there when you need them (and they're even there when you don't)."

It's "us" versus "them." I've heard well-meaning or sincere sponsors say something like, "They (your friends and relatives) don't believe because they don't understand." This is one of the oldest yet most effective tricks in the book. More than one network marketing organization is guilty of this type of cult-like "divide and conquer" activity.

Because the faithful have such a strong desire to believe, the clever sponsor can use such tactics as, "Anyone who is not for us is against us." "Don't listen to your family, friends, or relatives—they're just party poopers!" "What do they know, anyway?" "Are they driving a Lexus, Porsche, BMW, or Mercedes? If they aren't driving a luxury car, then why listen to them?"

To effectively control the faithful, the sponsor must cut them off from any "negative" contacts that they might encounter from "former" friends and family. Allegiance must be to the group and only to the group. Any threat to this loyalty must be wiped out and won't be tolerated.

If any network encourages you to ignore your family and

friends, or to cut them off completely, then run away as fast as you can and escape while you can. Your financial and/or even your physical life may depend upon this advice. More than one person who has ignored this warning has been destroyed not only financially, but also spiritually, emotionally, mentally, socially, or even physically.

> *Matthew 12:25: "Jesus knew their thoughts and said to them, 'Every kingdom divided against itself will be ruined, and every city or household divided against itself will not stand.'"*

Secret 13. The Victim

"Welcome to this week's episode of the blame game!"

Keep dreaming the dream! What? You didn't make it? Then you didn't dream hard enough" (in other words, "It's your own fault that you didn't make it—Loser!"). I'm no expert in psychology, but there seems to be little or no difference between "motivating the faithful" and "emotional manipulation" with network marketers. The victim didn't succeed, so blame the victim. Who likes to fail? Who likes to hang around a loser? People don't like to fail. I have observed that the fear of failure is often greater than the fear of anything else.

The fear of loss is a major motivator for most people. In some extreme cases, people would rather die than face the humiliation of failure. A clever sponsor will use the fear of failure as a subtle manipulation technique. "If you didn't 'make it,' then you didn't dream deeply enough." "It's your own fault—you should have invested more in yourself and purchased more of our special books, tapes, and videos on how to succeed." "You must not have believed enough in yourself." "I am not responsible for your success—you are." They promise you the world, but please look closely at that world before you buy into it.

The problem here is that most people don't succeed. It doesn't matter what network marketing company or program you choose, I can almost guarantee that over ninety percent of the people who have been associated with the company over the past twenty years are no longer there. In fact, although I don't even know you, I would have better than a seventy-five percent chance of being right on whether or not you could make it in ANY network marketing company or program.

Just because your family and friends have known you all of your life, they couldn't possibly know if you have what it takes to succeed in network marketing, right? Well, your family and friends will probably be even more accurate than I am in their assessments of your possibility for success and/or failure. In the probable event that you fail, they will most likely enjoy reminding you of this as often as possible, especially since most new recruits will fail in their network marketing attempts (nine out of ten with the previous example). Those odds aren't good.

The emotional damage of failure is deep and permanent. "I tried, but I failed..." "I really must be a loser..." "Yeah, they're right—I didn't sacrifice enough..." "I shouldn't have listened to all of those "party poopers" (who are now telling me 'I told you so!')..." "Non-believers are the real enemy here; yeah, that's the ticket..." "It couldn't be me, could it?"

Has one of the "faithful" in the flock fallen? Please make sure that you don't blame the victim even though it's what everyone else does that makes their living from network marketing. If you've tried networking and failed, then don't let them get the best of you. Most importantly make sure that you don't blame yourself for failing at a system that was stacked against you from the start!

Proverbs 15:4: "The tongue that brings healing is a tree of life, but a deceitful tongue crushes the spirit."

Proverbs 15:22: "Plans fail for lack of counsel, but with many advisers they succeed."

Chapter 4

Promotional Manipulation

Secret 14. The Tribal Story

"It really is a jungle out there..."

This product needs to use network marketing because _____ (fill in the blank with whatever story is behind it). In other words, "we couldn't sell this garbage any other way, so we decided to dump it on the market through a network marketing channel."

Network marketing programs are notorious for being overpriced. One review of a national network marketing leader found that, on the average, their products were much more expensive at suggested retail and slightly more expensive at distributor wholesale than comparable products at the regular price at the local store, mall, or supermarket. By the time you added back in the costs for shipping and handling, you are right back to where you started with a product that was way over priced. If you factor in all of the coupons plus other sales and incentives that are continually running at the store at any given moment, then the price differences become even more pronounced.

The network companies also promote themselves as replacing the middle man. Huh? Then who are the distributors—middle people? No, the truth is that the company that is jamming products down through the network channel is actually selling directly to the "final customer" because the "distributor" is really nothing more than "wholesale customer." Most distributors would never pass the retail sales test (selling to at least ten retail customers in the past thirty days), so this means that most distributors in these programs should really be reclassified as "wholesale customers" instead of "distributors." Even though the network marketing companies themselves will admit that a "wholesale only" business is illegal, few of them have moved to strictly enforce their retail sales policies.

Since so few products, if any, are actually ever sold at the suggested "retail price," this means that any promised commissions on retail sales is pure fantasy on the part of the network company. This takes away a major portion of the "promised" earnings capability of any network marketing program. When you take that away, a major source of incentive to participate is gone.

The sale of products is no longer a priority to most network marketers. What matters to them is building the channel. They call this "building people." Later it will be demonstrated that on the average, a distributor pays around four to six hundred dollars more out of his pocket per year for the privilege of being part of the distribution network than what he earns. Let's see—I pay you four to six hundred dollars more per year than what I make, and that's supposed to build me up. Wow! Sign me up and take my hard-earned money!

Jeremiah 22:13: "Woe to him who builds his palace by unrighteousness, his upper rooms by injustice, making his countrymen work for nothing, not paying them for their labor."

Secret 15. Hype

"...as sheep are led to the slaughter."

A few years back I sat in on a presentation where a sponsor stated, "We pay out ninety-eight percent back into the network in the form of bonuses and incentives!" Wow, sign these guys up!!! They need only two percent of the total "wholesale" sales to keep their company running. That is unbelievable! The Salvation Army is a non-profit charity, and they use only three percent of the funds donated to them for administration, etc. This person actually believed his audience would swallow the lie that his company was even more efficient and altruistic than the Salvation Army!

He was almost right because nobody at that event questioned the presenter on this point, except for me. I suddenly became *persona non-grata* for the balance of the meeting! I guess I should have learned by now that I should stop asking the hard questions at network marketing meetings.

"Clubs" and "trusts" are another area where deception is rampant. These sponsors would have their faithful believe that just because the main company doesn't keep the distributor's social security number on record that the government can't find them. Never mind that the company has the person's name, address, phone number, purchases, etc., on file.

It's baffling that well-educated, intelligent people lose their common sense when they walk through the door and gobble up this nonsense. I guess that the new rule for network marketing should be that "if it sounds too good to be true, then sign up immediately!"

> *Psalm 49:20: "A man who has riches without understanding is like the beasts that perish."*
>
> *Psalm 140:5: "Proud men have hidden a snare for me; they have spread out the cords of their net and have set traps for me along my path. Selah."*
>
> *Proverbs 1:17: "How useless to spread a net in full view of all the birds!"*

Secret 16. Tools

> *"Give me a lever with a long enough handle and I can move any distributor."*

CD's, audio tapes, video tapes, books, websites, meetings, rallies, and weekend seminars are the "tools" of the trade for the network marketer. If you really want to know how network marketing works, then follow the money trail. The money trail in this case leads to the understanding that tools are where the real money is made! Sponsors never become rich by selling only the products provided by the network marketing company. The big money is in selling tools such as books, tapes, videos, websites, rallies, weekend seminars, etc., that are aimed at motivating a person to "think positively" and supposedly teach the person how to succeed as a network marketer. Since over 90% of all people that have tried network marketing in the past have failed, then I guess that the tools just simply didn't work.

Again, it's important to understand what is meant by "think positively." In this case, "think positively" means that the faithful distributors will blindly purchase and subscribe to more and more tools. This helps ensure that the person who is producing the tools is making an adequate return on his investment in producing the tools. This is truly one of the darkest secrets of the network marketing industry and one key area that hasn't been fixed by either the companies or sponsors during the last two decades.

But why should they fix it? What on earth would ever motivate them to kill the goose that lays the golden egg and share the wealth? Sadly, as the last twenty years have demonstrated, there is no incentive whatsoever for the industry to fix this problem. Otherwise I wouldn't be writing this book, and the question wouldn't even be valid.

It wasn't until I reached the first major level in one of these programs that I realized that I was barely going to break even. What the heck happened to the promise of making an extra forty to sixty thousand dollars (or more) per year part-time? I guess that went out the window with the idea of selling the products at retail prices. If you don't sell at retail, then you don't earn a retail commission. It's that simple. My wife and I were going to be lucky if we barely supplemented our regular income at that point in time. Guess what happened? That's right. We found other ways to invest our time, money, and efforts.

Once I found out that the real money was in recruiting and in selling tools to these new recruits, and that I wouldn't get any commission on the sales of the tools, I became just a little bit annoyed. Since I wasn't the one producing the tools, then I wasn't the one who would benefit from selling the tools. Show me the money? Well, tools are where it's at! Sure, they showed me the money, but none of it was going to be coming my way anytime soon.

Let me see—I'm going to sell tens of thousands of dollars of "tools" for you each and every month and I'm not going to see a dime for my efforts. Hmmm, that doesn't make good marketing or business sense to me. In fact, this fails the most simple of all marketing tests because it doesn't give the right answer to the following question: "Hey, dude (sponsor, or whatever you're calling yourself this week), what's in it for me if I sell your tools to my friends, family and distributors?" The deafening silence screams back the answer: "Nothing!"

If the networking system you're trying to sell me can stand on its own and is as good as you claim, then why do I need to spend three thousand dollars every year on these "tools" to be successful? At one seminar they slapped the following propaganda up on the white board:

- If you join the right company...
- If you get the right training...
- If you have the right TOOLS...
- Then you *will* succeed.
- Others have. You can, too!

Wow! Tell me more! Do you mean that if I buy your tools, you will guarantee my success? Nope, sorry, can't do that. These "tool marketing" enterprises are for the complete benefit of the inner circle of people who are pushing the tools, not for the person purchasing the materials.

If these tools were as effective as they claimed, then why did I keep hearing my sponsor and uplines saying things like, "Oh, what do you mean that 'you didn't make it?' Then you just must not have *dreamed* hard enough." Their solution to my failure was that I should simply buy some more tapes, books, and videos. And by the way, "if you want to be really successful then you should also plan on attending a couple more weekend seminars and rallies so that you can continue to develop that *hidden talent* within." "One of these days you'll understand." "Understanding" usually occurs for the distributor at the same point in time when his wallet has been completely emptied.

One of the most startling statements I've heard in the past two decades was made by a top distributor of a well-known company at a distributor meeting. He said, "This is not a product business—it's a people business—helping to develop them." Don't misunderstand me—I'm all for professional training programs and have made a small fortune as a management consultant training top executives all over the globe.

What needs to be understood is what they really mean by "developing people." Their idea of "developing" people is to mine their minds and pocketbooks for cash. That's right, the giant sucking sound that you hear is the cash and credit being drained from your and other people's wallets and purses. I wonder if the network companies themselves would agree that it's not a product business. If it's not a product business, then why bother manufacturing anything? It just doesn't make any sense, does it?

The only value you have to your sponsor is your ability to put cash into their network and especially into their tool marketing enterprise. Once you stop buying the tools, then you can be certain that at first your sponsor's interest in you will go up quite a bit. They want to recapture the cash stream you were bringing in to their business. After the sponsor realizes that the end of your patience has been reached and that you're not going to spend any more money on worthless tools, then the sponsor's interest in you will fall off very quickly.

It all sounds so good to the casual observer, and it's communicated with such conviction and enthusiasm. But what you really need to ask your sponsor is, "Can you explain to me why it is that my sales of these 'tools' are never included in my networking sales volume?" Also, ask him, "Why don't I get a commission for selling these tools?" "How's that again, what's in it for me?" "Nothing?!" "Why not??!"

The truth is that if the tool marketing enterprise that produces the tapes, books, etc. were to let you in on the "success" of their tool system, then they would have to sacrifice a major portion of their annual income. In some cases, it has been reported that more than two-thirds or even more of these superstar's annual income is a result of tool sales, not due to the sales volume of the products that they are supposedly marketing. We're all one big happy family until you want a share of, or commission on, my tool sales volume. It is so simple. Don't expect to share in the profits from the sale of the tools.

"Are you already investing in yourself?" Are we "developing" nicely now? Oops, maybe I need to buy another tape to counteract my "bad" attitude!

A few years back an ad appeared in the classified section of a local newspaper. An ex-network marketer was selling out his "investment" of cassette and video tapes for the bargain basement price of one dollar each. Wow, this sounds like a great deal, right? Maybe, except that he had eight hundred tapes! He "invested" at least four thousand dollars, perhaps as much as sixteen thousand dollars, in "developing" himself. If he was so successful, then why was he selling off his entire investment in the very tools that he had used for his "development?" Didn't he succeed? It doesn't sound like it, does it? My guess is that he just didn't listen close enough to the tapes. I wonder how he feels about his "investment" in his development now. The backside of a donkey comes to mind.

Tools have become such a major problem for network marketing companies that one major company is now requiring all of its distributors to sign an arbitration agreement if they plan on promoting "sales tools" that have not been developed by the network marketing company itself. This is an implicit admission of guilt on the part of the company and an absolute confirmation that the system is broken and needs to be fixed. There's nothing like trying to shut the barn door after all of the Gullible Georges have already escaped.

> *James 5:4: "Look! The wages you failed to pay the workmen who mowed your fields are crying out against you. The cries of the harvesters have reached the ears of the Lord Almighty."*

Chapter 5

Sales and Marketing Plan Manipulation

Secret 17. Momentum and Critical Mass

"I think I can,
I thought I could;
oh well…"

There is a threshold that a network marketing company and every distributor must pass before either can survive. Until then, any bonus check that you get that you can cash at the bank is just frosting on the cake. In most cases, the critical mass is never reached, and the distributors are left with bouncing bonus checks and broken promises. I've seen Fred and Ned holding worthless bonus checks that were made out to them in the tens of thousands of dollars. The reason they couldn't cash the checks was that the network marketing company went bankrupt. That was a great bonus program, right? Too bad they couldn't cash the checks.

By the way, if anyone shows you a W–2 form for earnings from network marketing, it is probably illegal. Most network marketing companies have strict guidelines forbidding this practice. Also in this day and age, it is very easy to fabricate a realistic looking copy of either a W–2 or bonus check. All you need is a decent PC with a scanner and laser printer, and you're all set to create any façade that you want.

Remember Gary? Now here's a case study in "near success" and survival. One time, Gary almost succeeded big time. He had the national distribution rights for a concentrated, all natural product. This product was not just good—it was really good! It was all natural and processed in such a way that all of the natural flavors and benefits were retained. He had planned to use a distributor network to help him market the product. But first he worked the flea market and county fair circuits over a couple of summers. Then he went a more traditional route during one winter and was distributing the concentrated product in retail stores throughout the Midwest. Everything was going really well until spring and warmer weather arrived.

Did I mention that this was a preservative-free product? One day Gary got a call from one of his major customers who stored this product in a warehouse. "Gary, what are *WE* going to do?" "What do you mean, what are *WE* going to do?" Gary asked. The customer answered, "I've got your product everywhere. It's dripping off the rafters." (Kaboom!) You guessed it. The packages were exploding in the hot warehouse. It's amazing how far a little product can go on a hot, Midwest afternoon. By the time that Gary was finished paying for the cleanup of not just one warehouse, but many, he was lucky to be out of the concentrated, all natural product business for good without having to declare bankruptcy.

He had the momentum and had achieved critical mass, but just didn't anticipate his business being quite so explosive. Most network marketing companies will go the same way that the concentrated, all natural product business went. They end up growing too fast and then explode. It's usually the distributors who are left to clean up the resulting mess, which is usually a lot messier than a sticky, concentrated, all natural product.

The momentum for most downlines usually runs out six to ten levels below the first distributors who sign up. This is especially true of the scams where you buy the product only once at a price that's usually three times higher than the going market rate for the same product anywhere else. Eventually a level is reached where even the dumbest novice understands that there aren't any more saps left in the market to buy in to the program.

It's bad enough that the well-meaning novice distributors have probably already alienated all of their friends and family members already, but each and every time this happens to a network marketer, the industry loses just a little bit more credibility. How many times can people or companies reinvent themselves? Once a trust has been broken it is one of the most difficult things to repair.

> *Matthew 6:19–20: "Do not store up for yourselves treasures on earth, where moth and rust destroy, and where thieves break in and steal. But store up for yourselves treasures in heaven, where moth and rust do not destroy, and where thieves do not break in and steal."*

Secret 18. Being First

"First in, first out."

Those at the top *and who survive* make *all* the money. Where would you rather be: at the top or the bottom of the pyramid? Of course everyone wants to be at the top! If you're not in within the first few levels from the top, your chances for success and the big money are close to zero. This is common knowledge in the network marketing industry.

Once the organizational structure is in place, the channel is created through which more and more of the product can be pushed. It's a combination of maximizing the quantity of distributors (customers) with the largest volume of product purchases possible per distributor. This is why one of the co-founders of one company said with complete confidence: "We'll expand our business not just by selling more per 'store' but by opening more 'stores,'" or in other words, drafting more distributors or wholesale customers. Isn't it amazing how quickly the "stores" open and close?

The main roads, side streets, and detours in life are littered with the remains of people's broken "dreams" and those people have simply ended up as network marketing casualties. The list is incredibly long and we are now talking in terms of tens of millions of people that have been crushed by the network marketing machine. If the sponsor is truly "helping" other people help themselves, then why are there so many broken, bitter, and self-deceived dreamers smashed by the side of the road? It's important to keep in mind that the person that the sponsor is helping is himself, not you.

Proverbs 14:23: "All hard work brings a profit,
but mere talk leads only to poverty."

Matthew 20:16: "So the last will be first, and the first will be last."

Secret 19. Cross Network Competition

"Let the 'cross network' games begin!"

All of the other distributors who are in the same network marketing program as you are NOT your allies; they are your competitors and, therefore your enemies. You had better have a significant competitive advantage over them if you're going to beat them out and succeed. If you have no major competitive advantage, pack your bags, because you've already lost the battle. Most people don't seem to have the street smarts to really grasp what's happening.

As other people's networks grow, your chances of building a network decrease proportionally to the increase in the overall size of those other networks. This is why so many tool marketing enterprises have sprung up. There is a huge need to create the illusion of a competitive advantage for each "independent" network; otherwise there is little or no hope of succeeding in this business. What is the key thing that the networks use to prove they have a competitive advantage? That's right, tools! Our group ABC's tools are far more superior to team XYZ's tools. Really? Then why do more than half of all the distributors quit each year?

The only chance that the sponsor has is to create confusion in the marketplace and hope that the recruits leave their brains and convictions at the door when they walk in and that they'll let greed take over. If the new recruit refuses to buy in to the fantasy that everyone is part of one big happy family, then the game is already over.

*Psalm 69:4: "Those who hate me without rea-
son outnumber the hairs of my head; many are
my enemies without cause, those who seek to
destroy me. I am forced to restore what I did not
steal."*

Secret 20. The List

*"Write down everyone you know on a piece of paper:
friends, family, neighbors, your doctor, lawyer,
hairdresser, beautician, vet, pastor, priest, rabbi,
small business owner, sports figure, actor, actress,
reporter, writer, you name it, you write it down..."*

One of the strengths of network marketing is the
power of the "list" and the prospect's complete loyalty to the "system." The sponsor has already profiled the
prospect and put him on his list. Long before database marketing had become the norm in traditional businesses, successful network marketers were applying this principle. By
focusing on and managing "the list," a sponsor is able to get
maximum effect out of his efforts. In today's world, this is a
best-of-class business practice.

Successful network marketers are usually very intelligent
people and will use this type of technology to their advantage. A little bit of knowledge in the wrong hands really is a
dangerous thing to everyone around them. It's the sponsors
who do the most damage here. Don't let them fool you.
They may act "down-to-earth," but you will end up being the
one trampled down into the earth.

One-to-one marketing is also one of the latest and greatest
buzzwords. One-to-one marketing changes the perspective to
"What share of the customer's mind do you have (ten, forty,

or seventy-five percent)?" It would be wise to ask your sponsor, "What is the probability that you can convert someone over to purchasing 100 percent of their consumables from just one source, that is, from only you (especially if it's going to cost that person more money to be involved in the long run)?" My answer is slim to none unless you can "convert" the person into a "new" way of life. If you do that, then it's easy to move a lot of tools and product through the channel.

> *Numbers 1:2: "Take a census of the whole Israelite community by their clans and families, listing every man by name, one by one."*

Secret 21. Body Count

> *"I am not a distributor; I am a human development specialist!"*

Network marketing companies are no longer product driven; they are "people" driven. But, if you talk with the networking companies directly, they will claim that theirs are "product" businesses. Actions speak louder than words, and if this were true, then the companies would have moved long ago to clean up the mess they've created. It has all become a numbers game.

Fill the pipeline with enough new recruits, and the rest will take care of itself. This sounds simple enough until you've run out of "new" recruits. It doesn't take very long to exhaust your list of friends and family. Usually the new distributor has burned through that list and those relationships within the first month or so.

As mentioned earlier, fifty percent of all distributors will quit the program each and every year. If I'm a distributor trying to build a business, I don't want to have to replace half of my distributor/customer base every year. What's the point? Worse yet, what a pain! Are you really willing to make the sacrifices necessary to succeed? If you do succeed, will you have any peace in the end?

How many broken dreams and relationships will you leave in your wake in your pursuit of success? How many of your original friends and family will still want to "get together for a cup of coffee and chat" anymore? At first the "social aspect" helps fuel the body count, but in the end it leaves a long, sorry trail of dead bodies in the dust.

> *Proverbs 14:12: "There is a way that seems right to a man, but in the end it leads to death."*

> *Proverbs 14:20: "The poor are shunned even by their neighbors, but the rich have many friends."*

Secret 22. The Formula

"Let's see, 2 times 2 equals $1 million—really!"

The formula is this simple: warm bodies in; cold stiffs out. Marketing is war, and it's the front line troops in the trenches that are expendable. Most network marketing companies have huge attrition rates (the number of distributors that quit each year). But they know that the bigger the army that they have, the better chance they have for survival. Without that critical mass, they cannot survive the loss of so many of their troops each and every year.

So it really doesn't matter to the companies if nearly half of the distributors who are registered with them worldwide will probably drop out in the course of a year. By sheer force of numbers it is possible to survive, but at what cost? What good is it to gain all the material wealth in the world if you end up selling out your principles?

Statistical formulas are also applied to the sale of audio tapes, video tapes, books, and meetings. Network marketers can now predict, within a very tight range, what kind of success you will experience by how many tools are being sold through your network. The more recruits you have, the more tools you can sell. The more tools you sell, the more money your sponsor's upline will make.

They want us to believe them when they say, "All of this success can be yours for only a couple of extra hours of your time per week." If it's such a great opportunity, then why are people jumping off the program like rats off a sinking ship?

Proverbs 11:1: "The LORD abhors dishonest scales, but accurate weights are his delight."

Secret 23. Dilution

"Anyone can drink a liter of arsenic, as long as it's been diluted with tens of thousands of liters of pure water and drunk over a twenty-year time span."

Very often, the new network marketer must swear absolute allegiance to his or her sponsor, upline and company to be successful. This is probably partly true because participating in more than one network marketing program at a time will lead to fast failure on the part of the distributor due to a dilution of their effort.

But on the other hand, since each and every distributor is an independent business person they should be able to represent the products and companies that best meet the needs of their customer group. The problem for the sponsors is that if their distributors are participating in other networks, then their efforts will be diluted and they'll lose the leverage of your network and your pocketbook.

Currently it is estimated that some seven million people are active in various network marketing plans in the U.S. With more than two hundred network marketing companies all competing for the same mindshare and wallets, that means that less than thirty-five thousand distributors, on the average, are available to each company. There is a finite universe of people who are willing to participate in these programs, and the upper limits have now been reached in the U.S. market.

Remember Fred and Ned? They're easily on the bandwagon of three to four new companies every year. The problem here is that there is no way to keep the Gullible Georges of the world from getting excited about "another innovative and electrifying program" three, four, or even a dozen times each and every year. Dilution and churn are inevitable in any networking organization. They create the need for warm bodies in, cold bodies out, and retaining customers isn't even discussed, much less pursued. Again, nobody has really figured out how to capture customers for life in the network marketing industry.

One other area of dilution occurs when a distributor is not there to build the networking business, but rather is there to build his professional practice. I've observed doctors, lawyers, accountants, and other professionals who have stayed with particular network marketing programs for years. At first I was baffled as to why they would do this. But then it was clear that they were there to build their own professional practices from the flow of new recruits who were parading through the network marketing programs.

It's the same idea as joining the Rotary or Chamber of

Commerce. By joining the network marketing programs, they increased their chances that they would meet new and different groups of people. Also, by doing this they were able to reduce their cost of acquiring new customers into the professional businesses where they really made their living. Chances are that even long after a person dropped out of the network marketing program, he or she was probably still using the services of the professional. While this was a great tactic on the part of the professionals involved, it really didn't do much to build the sponsor's network.

Isaiah 1:22: "Your silver has become dross, your choice wine is diluted with water."

Secret 24. Overlap

"How many network marketers can you share and still survive?"

There is a tendency for distributor overlap between companies. Every time that I hear about another network company that has reached the magic number of 100,000 distributors, I chuckle. It's all part of the hype (faking it and making it) to drive the start-up company to their next level of success. As more network companies enter the marketplace, more and more overlap will take place between them. It becomes a vicious circle. Ultimately it will be the network marketers themselves who will end up being the big losers.

Overlap also occurs with products and tools. How many products can a salesperson effectively represent? How many products can a salesperson sell and still be successful? I know that the answer to these questions is probably more than one or two. But, I also know that it is far, far less than the 5,000+ products that some companies have in their product lines!

Network marketing companies know and understand that the faithful must not waste their efforts on other networking programs. At the same time, these same companies jam all of the products that they possibly can down through the channels (distributors). In the end, the overlap takes place internally as well as externally. And how do you spell burnout?

> *Psalm 57:6: "They spread a net for my feet—I was bowed down in distress. They dug a pit in my path—but they have fallen into it themselves. Selah."*

> *Proverbs 12:15: "The way of a fool seems right to him, but a wise man listens to advice."*

Secret 25. Market Limits

"Big ideas in a shrinking market..."

A trend by network marketing companies is to try to apply the idea that there are no market limitations to the network marketing industry. They are trying to sell the idea that your market limit has not been reached until you have sold your product to every person in your potential market. The network marketers want you to believe that until everyone in the world has purchased the products that you're selling, there is still market share available for you to capture. All that it takes is a little investment of time on your part.

The mathematical theories that can be used to prove market limitations are basically correct. Unfortunately, as soon as you enter the real world, you can throw all of the nice, tight mathematical formulas out the window. Business reality and mathematics rarely occupy the same space at the same time. As soon as you put people into the equation, all bets are off.

Let's crunch some more numbers together and assume that a networking company has one million distributors in the U.S. In that case, this means that there is one distributor for every 260 people (every man, woman, and child in the U.S.). What do you think the likelihood of any "independent" business surviving with a market size that averages only 260 customers per "store"? My guess is that there aren't many stores that could survive with those kinds of odds.

Network marketing sponsors desperately rely upon the faithful believing that there is still market share for them to capture in their home country. "The only limits to your local market are the constraints that you place on yourself and in your mind." They claim that "you can still make it here," when the reality is that the only place that the program itself is experiencing any real growth is in new international markets. International expansion is great for the network marketing company and sponsors because there is a whole new world of converts waiting to be won over in the name of free enterprise and economic evangelism.

Proverbs 23:4: "Do not wear yourself out to get rich; have the wisdom to show restraint."

Secret 26. Saturation

"At some point in time, you run out of suckers."

71

How many levels deep would someone have to go to sponsor every man, woman, and child in America? Only nineteen levels—using a four-by-four matrix! "What do you mean you can't sponsor anyone?" "If you fail, it is because you didn't dream hard enough, didn't work hard enough," and on and on it goes.

I've been told along the way, in many of the seminars that I've attended, that one out of five people can be successfully trained as a salesperson. If this is true, then the total potential market for network marketing programs are just over fifty million people. That is the total pool of sales resources available to fill every sales position in every company in America! If you subtract the seven million people already involved in network marketing, that leaves around forty-three million or so potential salespeople available for the rest of the companies in the U.S. This seems to be a reasonably sized market in which to grow a network marketing business, but it isn't.

With over seven million people currently active in network marketing organizations in the U.S., that means one out of every thirty-eight people in America is already involved in a network marketing company! Sorry, but you've got better odds of winning the Lotto than of becoming a network marketing millionaire with numbers like that. Tell me, can any "independent" business survive with a pool of only thirty-eight potential distributors, on the average? Somebody, somewhere, is getting the shaft—and it's the poor distributor at the bottom of the pyramid.

If the attrition rate in the network marketing industry was only twenty percent per year (which is being more than generous since it is actually over fifty percent), then that means that 1.4 million people will quit the network marketing industry each year. In just ten years, fourteen million people will have quit. That's double the amount of people that are currently involved in network marketing! Even worse, one in three of every potential salesperson in America will have been in and out of network marketing within a decade.

If the pros or people with natural sales talent can't make it, what makes you think that you can? Sure, some of you will make it, but you will be the exception, not the rule. If you happen to be the exception to the rule and actually succeed in network marketing, then I would suggest that you would have succeeded in ANY sales effort, whether it was networking, real estate sales, insurance sales, or whatever.

What the sponsors always neglect to tell the distributors is that once critical mass has been achieved, it's not long until a type of "saturation" of the market occurs. This isn't the "mathematical" saturation point, but rather it's a saturation point in the mind of the prospect, customer, and distributor. In reality, the saturation point in the prospect's mind seldom reaches the highest level due to the fact that almost half of all "distributors" or "customers," or whatever you want to call them, leave the program every year. Therefore, there is always a fresh set of old and new distributors and/or customers who are just waiting to be claimed or reclaimed. At least, that is what they're hoping you will believe. Why else would anyone want or agree to work with something that is such a "hard sell?"

It doesn't matter what product is being marketed, sooner or later once critical mass is achieved, then the attrition rate becomes a major headache for the people who are legitimately trying to make the system work. It's not very effective CRM (customer relationship management) to have to be replacing your entire customer and/or distributor base every two years or so. As it was demonstrated earlier in this book, the cost of customer acquisition in the network marketing industry is staggering, and conducting business this way cannot be very efficient in the long term. Perhaps this inefficiency is one of the main reasons that the network marketing companies are forced to charge higher wholesale and retail prices as compared to other competitive products.

> *Proverbs 23:5: "Cast but a glance at riches, and they are gone, for they will surely sprout wings and fly off to the sky like an eagle."*

Chapter 6

Financial Manipulation

Secret 27. Debt

"I owe, I owe, it's off to a rally I go..."

Keep your distributors in debt to motivate them to succeed. Force them to burn their means of escape. The average distributor for one particular company here in the U.S. will net around eight hundred dollars a year in bonuses and markups from selling products for that company. But, in addition to the products the distributor sells to others, he will also consume, on average, twelve hundred dollars worth of goods and services himself.

This doesn't even take into consideration the hundreds or even thousands of dollars more that will be spent on telephone bills, gasoline for the car, tickets to rallies, publicity materials, and other expenses to grow their business. So let's see now, I spent twelve hundred dollars to make eight hundred dollars. Makes sense to me, how about you? Personally, it makes more sense to go join a wholesale club for $25 and pocket the other $375!

Some of the distributors may end up dipping into their savings, and a few may even run up substantial personal debts (credit cards, lines of credit, etc.). Some people have even gone bankrupt. People end up with so much skin in the game that they can't afford to back out. It's almost like slot machines at the casino. "Maybe if I keep pouring money into this box, I'll get some of my investment back." It can really become a twisted addiction for some. Each year when it's time to renew their distributorships, they think, "Maybe this year will be different." Maybe they should be asking themselves, "How will it be different this time around?"

The real crime here is that many of the people pouring themselves into this business are the ones who can least afford to do so. That two-hundred-dollar startup kit (and tools) may be pocket change for the people at the top of the pyramid, but to those at the bottom, it may represent their entire life's savings. *Free Enterprise* is definitely not free and those that borrow to finance their activities are setting themselves up for a major disappointment in the end.

> *Proverbs 22:26–27: "Do not be a man who strikes hands in pledge or puts up security for debts; if you lack the means to pay, your very bed will be snatched from under you."*

Secret 28. Desperation

"Pursuing dreams in quiet desperation."

Don't try to question whether or not you can make money or not. It really doesn't matter that the average distributor earns an average of only around sixty-five dollars per month, or around eight hundred dollars per year. To get to the first major milestone of success in a network marketing company, you need approximately eighty customers or distributors in your organization averaging two hundred dollars per month in purchases or sales.

That means that for every distributor in America to go to the first major level of success, then over eighty million people would need to be involved as either customers or distributors (there are currently somewhere just over one million distributors for this particular company in America). If you remember the numbers from earlier, the total market that is really available for your network marketing plan is only around a maximum of forty-five million salespeople, so that means we're already thirty-five million people short! If you really want to see the fireworks fly, then pin down your would-be sponsor on this point. He'll have a meltdown. The reality and the numbers are simple.

Another thing that the general public is not usually aware of is that most network marketing companies do not follow GAAP when reporting sales figures. They report their sales at distributor retail, not at wholesale (the price at which they really sell the products). So, if they reported over $7 billion in sales, the real number was actually around $2.8 billion in sales to distributors. Why is it necessary for them to misrepresent their sales figures? What's the point of this façade?

When you factor in the two million distributors worldwide, that is an average of only around fourteen hundred dollars per year per distributor in wholesale sales (remember that most distributors rarely sell at retail, if ever). The numbers are stacked against the distributors from the start. In the end, desperate distributors with "big" dreams will beg, borrow, or steal to be in "at the top" of the next great opportunity, and that is truly pathetic.

Ecclesiastes 2:11: "Yet when I surveyed all that my hands had done and what I had toiled to achieve, everything was meaningless, a chasing after the wind; nothing was gained under the sun."

Chapter 7

Master
Manipulation

Secret 29. Greed

"Making money, making money!"

As long as people love money more than anything, there will always be room for network marketing, especially if it's a well-financed scheme wrapped in a multi-billion dollar air of credibility and topped off with God, family, and country.

Greed is the one secret that is hidden out in the open by all network marketing firms. How can rational people truly believe that if they invest one, two, eight, or even twenty hours per week in their (part-time) "venture" that they will really become rich beyond their wildest dreams?

Remember the questions about time and money that are asked? Who isn't susceptible to greed? Who doesn't want to be a millionaire? Greed is the green-eyed monster that spews discontent and causes otherwise rational people to behave quite foolishly. By the time they come to their senses, they end up kicking themselves for having been so naive. It is not without reason that one of the wisest men to ever live wrote:

> *Proverbs 15:27: "A greedy man brings trouble to his family, but he who hates bribes will live."*

Solomon also wrote:

> *Ecclesiastes 5:10: "Whoever **loves** money never has money enough; whoever **loves** wealth is never satisfied with his income. This too is meaningless." (Emphasis added.)*

Greed starts from the top and trickles down throughout the entire network. When the companies try to claim that they are not to blame, this is a lie. Most of the people that start the network marketing companies also sponsor themselves into the network at the very top layer to ensure that a lion's share of the network profits are diverted into their own pockets. Some have even created additional corporate entities to hide the fact that they're doing this. Since the duplication within a network occurs from the top down, there is absolutely no way that the network marketing companies can shift the blame to other people further down in the organization.

"Meaningless" is the word that hits the nail on the head. The network marketing sponsors have understood all too well that it's true that people love money more than anything, and they have leveraged the secret power of greed to create vast empires. It is so sad that greed, as an ethic, has become good and acceptable. Last time I checked, "The LOVE of money really is the root of all evil."

*Luke 16:13–14: "'No servant can serve two masters. Either he will hate the one and love the other, or he will be devoted to the one and despise the other. You cannot serve both God and Money.' The Pharisees, who **loved** money, heard all this and were sneering at Jesus." (Emphasis added.)*

*1 Timothy 6:10: "For the **love** of money is a root of all kinds of evil. Some people, eager for money, have wandered from the faith and pierced themselves with many griefs." (Emphasis added.)*

Secret 30. When All Else Fails, Change Your Name

"Call it whatever you want, but a network marketing company is still a network marketing company, even if they want you to believe that they're something new and improved."

For every MLM or network marketing company that is in the "MLM graveyard," there are more that have popped up to take its place. Sometimes it's the same company that pops up in a new set of clothes for the emperor. The only problem is that the clothes the emperor has bought are invisible, and even a child can see through them. For example, there is a subtle, yet enlightening, reorganization and repositioning of the brand that is taking place at Amway right before your eyes. Amway is no longer the "big dog" in the DeVos and Van Andel family of businesses. It is now a subsidiary of Alticor. From the Alticor website it is stated that:

Alticor and its subsidiaries, Access Business Group, Amway and Quixtar, generate annual sales of more than $4 billion. Alticor also owns a Grand Rapids, Mich., landmark, the Amway Grand Plaza Hotel. Alticor provides leadership and support to these businesses, from strategic direction to corporate services. Its Pyxis Innovations division develops new products, services and businesses. Alticor and its subsidiaries are privately held by the DeVos and Van Andel families.

The negative baggage that is associated with the Amway "brand" and name has finally caused the DeVos and Van Andel families to admit that is was time regroup and rename "the business." Even the Amway distributors themselves cringe when a prospect asks them, "Is this Amway?" Most of the distributors have been trained to deceive the prospect and tell them, "No, this is Quixtar." Or they might substitute one of the sub-brands such as Artistry for Quixtar. When your own network of distributors intuitively understands that they have to mitigate the negative baggage associated with a brand, then it is time for a change.

Alticor has even decided that the Access Business Group will be allowed to private label even short production runs for non-Alticor products. Is that just "good business"? Yes it is, especially if you need to get full utilization of your manufacturing facilities. My personal interpretation is that things have sunk so low overall for Alticor that it needs to resort to these kinds of measures to prop up the return on investment (ROI) for the production facilities.

It wasn't so long ago that they reported sales of over $7 billion! Now they're down to $4 billion. As pointed out earlier, this means that they have dropped from estimated wholesale sales of $2.8 billion (on the $7 billion) to $1.6

billion (on the $4 billion in "sales"). That has got to hurt when your sales drop by over forty percent during any given time period! This also means that they have a lot of idle production capacity that is not being used to its fullest.

One of the keys in manufacturing is to keep the utilization rate of your production plants as high as possible. That's the only way to get the largest ROI. Oh yeah, I forgot—they're not in the "product" business anymore; they're in the "people" business. What's the point of producing a product if you're not in the product business anymore? I guess that's why their production plant utilization rates have been suffering.

All network marketing companies, sooner or later, will confront the same problems that Amway has had to confront. How do you repair the ill will of twenty million people? How do you recapture the hearts and minds of people that you've offended so deeply over the past forty years that they never want to have anything to do with your business again? Changing your name is one option, and it wouldn't surprise me if the Amway "brand" actually disappeared sometime in the near future. However, even if Amway does disappear as a brand, it doesn't repair the root causes of the problem or the damage that has been done. It's a superficial change at best or a sad self-deception at worst. The market has a long memory, especially when it was burned by any particular brand.

Proverbs 16:18: "Pride goes before destruction, a haughty spirit before a fall."

Matthew 16:26: "What good will it be for a man if he gains the whole world, yet forfeits his soul? Or what can a man give in exchange for his soul?"

Post Mortem

People, if nothing else, please be brutally honest with yourself if you are even considering network marketing as a part- or full-time career. If you can't be brutally honest with yourself, then find a friend who will be. If you have no friends left, then contact me. In that case I'll be more than happy to be brutally honest with you.

If you are still going to insist on joining a network marketing company, then do us both a favor and send me the money instead. I'll be happy to solve your need to part with your hard earned money—so just send it to me (no cash please—checks and money orders only), and I'll be happy to spend it for you.

If you don't want to send your money to me, then at least do yourself the favor of using the "evaluating network marketing programs" that's included in the next section of this book. If by some chance the network marketing company that you're considering can pass this test, then join it.

For the rest of you, even if I end up helping just one person by writing this book and have saved him or her from losing countless thousands of dollars, then I will have truly succeeded.

> *Galatians 6:7: "Do not be deceived: God cannot be mocked. A man reaps what he sows."*

PART II

EVALUATING NETWORK MARKETING PROGRAMS

Evaluating a Networking or MLM "Opportunity"

If you are truly intent on pursuing a career in this industry, then you'll want to ask and get the answers to a series of questions such as the ones that I've used in the past and are included in this section. These questions are probably tainted with my bias toward network marketing in general, but they hit the key issues that you need to find out. Network marketing sponsors who are intimidated by this line of questioning will resort to ridicule or sarcasm to try and downplay the importance of your getting the REAL answers to these questions. Shining bright lights in dark corners will bring out the strangest reactions in people.

If your potential sponsor cannot, or will not, openly and honestly answer these questions to the best of his or her ability, then do yourself a favor and just say, "No thank you" to the "opportunity." It may be that not all of these questions will apply to every network marketing scheme that exists, but you should be able to have a relatively sound evaluation by the time you've gotten the answers to these questions.

Company Evaluation: The 30 Questions a Sponsor Hopes to Never Hear

Questions about "tools" (books, tapes, videos, meetings, seminars and rallies)

1. What tools are provided to help me do this business?
   - Does this group have its own set of exclusive tools?
   - Am I required to purchase books, cassette tapes or videos in order to participate in this program?
   - Is attendance at weekly meetings, seminars and rallies mandatory?
   - Do these tools guarantee that I'll have an advantage over the other distributor groups?

2. If my group of distributors purchases US$100,000 per year in "tools," then what will my commission be?
   - What is my commission on $500,000 in sales of tools?
   - What is my commission on $1,000,000 in sales of tools?
   - How much should I expect to have to invest in myself to be successful?
   - What is the average amount each of your distributors spends each month "investing" in themselves?

3. What is the commission structure for tools sold to the distributors that sign-up under me?
   - If there is no commission structure for selling tools, then why is that?

4. Since I'm not receiving any commission on the sales of these tools, then can you please explain what's in it for me?
   - What is my incentive for pushing your books, tapes, videos, meetings, seminars and rallies through my organization?
   - If I have 500 people in my group each purchasing $1,000 per year in tools for a total of $500,000 per year, then why shouldn't I (and my team of distributors) receive commissions on those sales? If not, why not?

5. If the marketing plan you just demonstrated to me is able to stand on its own, why do I need to purchase more tools in order to succeed?
   - Are your tools approved by the main company? If not, why not?

6. If I invest in myself and fail, then doesn't that mean that your tools failed and were inferior? If not, why not?
   - Do you guarantee my success in your program if I purchase your tools?
   - Is there a 100% money back (no questions asked) satisfaction guarantee on these tools? If not, why not?
   - Will I get all of my money refunded with no questions asked? If not, why not?

7. What businesses, organizations or groups, outside your network of distributors, use these tools to build their businesses?
   - Can you give me 10 (or for that matter, any) references of companies outside of your network that are using these tools to successfully build their business?

8. There are a number of professionally done sales & marketing tools that have been created by top performers from all kinds of industries, is there anything preventing me from packaging and marketing my own set of tools?
   - Or is there the expectation that I buy tools exclusively from your group?
   - What do I get in exchange for this exclusivity?
   - What happens if I refuse to use your tools and materials?
   - Does the network marketing company require that I sign an arbitration agreement if I want to produce, use and sell my own tools? If so, why?

Legal Questions

9. Am I protected from legal damages in the case that one of the products or tools sold either hurts someone or damages someone else's property?
   - How much liability insurance is carried per distributor?
   - If none, then how much should I plan on spending to obtain that type of protection for my independent business?

10. How many lawsuits have there been (or currently are in process) against the main company?
   - How many distributors have sued?
   - Have they collected damages? If so, what is the largest amount that has been awarded to these distributors by the courts?
   - Has the company been sued regarding tools?

11. Has the government investigated, or is currently investigating, your company?
   - If so, why?
   - If a case is no longer pending, what was the final outcome?

12. Have any distributors been subject to lawsuits or action by other distributors or by local, state or federal authorities?
   - If so, why?
   - If a case is no longer pending, what was the final outcome?

Product and Pricing Questions

13. Does the money-back guarantee extend to both distributors and retail customers?
    - If it only applies to retail customers, then am
      I expected to absorb the loss associated with
      product returns from unhappy customers? If
      so, why?
    - What is the percentage of total sales that
      should be expected as product returns?

14. Your product's retail prices don't seem to be in line
with market prices for similar, competitive products,
can you explain why that is?
    - Does the company provide, at no expense to
      the distributor, comparisons against all lead-
      ing brands (to account for the price/quan-
      tity/quality differences)? If not, why not?
    - What types of regional/national advertising is
      used to support the overall sales effort?
    - How much is spent on TV, Print, Radio, etc.
      in support of distributor activities?

15. Can you provide me a list of ten people that have purchased and continue to purchase these products at retail?
    - If not, why not?
    - How many personal, retail customers do you
      have?
    - What are their average monthly purchases?

16. What level of retail sales should I expect?
    - Can I effectively represent ALL products
      offered?
    - What is the largest number of separate prod-
      ucts sold by any single distributor?

- How much investment of both time and money will be required for me to effectively represent each and every product?
- What are the average annual product purchases made by distributors?
- What are the average annual sales per distributor?
- What portion of those sales are retail sales?
- What portion of those sales are wholesale sales?

Income Questions

17. If, on the average, the distributors spend more on purchases than they receive in annual commissions and bonuses, can you explain to me why that is happening?
    - In other words, how much money should I plan on investing above and beyond the monthly income that I receive? For example, for phone calls, gas, mileage, weekend seminars, hotel costs, rallies and the like?

18. What percentages of all recruits achieve the income levels that were shown in the examples that were given?
    - In other words, what percentage of all recruits actually makes a decent living in this program?
    - Can you give me 10 references that I can call and verify this information with them? If not, why not?

Positioning Questions

19. Is the product that is being sold or building people the most important part of this business?
    - If the product is most important, how much training will be required for me to market and sell these products?
    - If building people is the most important, can you please explain to me, then, how this program isn't just another pyramid or "Ponzi" scheme?

20. What is the competitive advantage of your group?
    - Why should I join your group?
    - What special advantage do I have joining your particular organization versus any other group in the same company?
    - I have a _____ (brother, sister, nephew, niece, aunt, uncle, cousin, etc., you fill in the blank) that is already in the program – shouldn't I be loyal to them and sign up under them in order that they benefit from the income generated from my downline? Why not?

21. What is the overall competitive advantage of the company and program?
    - Are the products truly better quality?
    - Does *"Consumer's Reports"* (or some other independent group) have comparisons available between your products and the competition? If not, why not?
    - Do you personally use ALL of the products offered by your company (every last one of them)? If not, why not?

22. What kind of attention is the media giving your company?
    - What kind of negative press is the company getting?
    - What kind of positive press is the company receiving?
    - What mixed signals are the company sending out?

23. What kind of assurance can you give me that I will succeed if I join your program?
    - Do I have the credibility, both personally and professionally, to succeed in this business?
    - Or will it be necessary for me to create an artificial image in order to succeed? In other words, do I have to "fake it till I make it?"
    - Do I have the skill, ability and background to duplicate my success?

Organizational Questions

24. What percentage of all new recruits actually make it to the top of the pyramid?
    - What percentage of all recruits make it to even the middle?

25. How many other distributors am I competing against?
    - How many distributors do you have in your group?
    - How many distributors are there in the company as a whole?
    - Is the market saturated already? If not, why not?

26. What happens if none of my friends, family or relatives sign-up for the program?
    - Does the company provide leads on prospects?
    - Does your group provide leads on prospects?

27. How important are my relationships to my family and friends?
    - How will this business change those relationships?
    - Am I prepared to sacrifice those relationships?
    - Does your group encourage people to ignore the advice of family and friends? If so, why?
    - Does this program require 100% allegiance from me, at the expense of my relationships to my family, friends and relatives?

28. What is the distributor attrition rate for this opportunity?
    - How many distributors leave or quit your group each year?
    - How many distributors leave the entire program each year?
    - What is the percentage split of new versus old distributors that leave each year?
    - How often will I have to replace my entire distributor base?
    - Every year?
    - Every other year?
    - Every third year?

29. What is the retail customer attrition rate?
    - How many retail customers leave or quit your group each year?

- How often will I have to replace my entire retail customer base?
- Every year?
- Every other year?
- Every third year?

30. Does your network use a "don't tell them who we are" tactic or the "curiosity approach when recruiting new people?"
    - What technique was used in setting up the initial appointment (not telling you what it was about, etc.)?
    - If an evasive technique was used, why? What are you hiding?
    - Why are you so evasive in dealing with the tough questions?
    - Finally, are there any other names that your network company has had during its entire history?

OK, so there were actually around 115 questions, but I just got so caught up in the moment that I did exactly opposite of what the network marketers typically do—I delivered more value for your money than you expected (or were promised)!

Part III

FAÇADE LINE INTERNATIONAL

Case Study: Façade Line International

Here's how the ultimate network marketing company works: you buy your own success with Façade Line International - don't be afraid to purchase your own level of achievement! Why waste your time with meetings, books, tapes and videos when you can buy the success that you deserve?

But wait! There's more!! You can offer your friends and acquaintances this amazing 'OPPORTUNITY,' too. All you have to do is invite them over for cup of coffee (or espresso) and make them believe that you're really interested in them on a social level. If this 'method' proves useless, LIE!

The first way you make MONEY with Façade Line International is that you need bodies (warm or cold) to get suckered into your NETWORK! One of Façade Line International's more popular books on this subject is Prospects Unaware: How to Get an Unsuspecting Prospect to believe that he/she is coming to a social event.

Building the network is Façade Line International's primary business and once you've signed-up as an official Façade Line Distributor you can then buy distributorships from Façade Line International at a 50% discount. How do you make money? Resell the distributorships (for whatever you can get) to your brother-in-law, mother-in-law, cousin, or whoever else you can snooker into this. You never need to worry about bonus checks again because you make all of your money up-front with us.

It is to your greatest advantage to sponsor your new recruits into your network as Sham Rock distributors. There is only one rule when it comes to sponsoring new recruits: you can not sponsor a distributor in at a higher level than what you are. For example, if you're only a Bogus Red, you can only sponsor other Bogus Reds or Sham Simples (ah, simplicity in complexity). The following are products (with the "S" product codes) and prices for each level in this fantastic program:

S-00001 Sham Simple (1st level distributor) $25.00
S-00002 Bogus Red (2nd level distributor) $50.00
S-00003 Pseudo Bead (3rd level distributor) $75.00
S-00004 Cubic Zirco (4th level distributor) $100.00
S-00005 Sham Rock (5th level distributor) $125.00

The other way you make MONEY with Façade Line International is to SELL Façade Line International's exclusive line of PRODUCTS. Let's begin with the Façade Line International Image Enhancement line of products.

Once you have "achieved" your desired level of success in Façade Line International, it is essential to project the proper "image" to all of your friends and relatives (if you have any left). Therefore the Façade Line International façade line of products helps you imitate it until you achieve it. Need to take a picture of yourself in front of a luxury or sports car? Or, do you need to show off your latest vacation in the Caribbean? (But never seem to have the money, time, or both to pull off the façade)? Now you can buy the "look" you need and desire:

S-00006 Dream House Façade
S-00007 Island Villa Façade
S-00008 Luxury Car Façade
S-00009 Sports Car Façade
S-00010 Sport Utility Vehicle Façade
S-00011 Sailing Yacht Façade
S-00012 Power Yacht Façade
S-00013 Yacht Club Façade
S-00014 Caribbean Cruise Façade
S-00015 English Butler Façade
S-00016 French Maid Façade
S-00017 Celebrity Friend Façade
S-00018 Business Jet Façade
S-00019 Jet Helicopter Façade
S-00020 Tennis Club Façade
S-00021 Teak Office Suite Façade
S-00022 Home Office Façade
S-00023 Country Club Façade
S-00024 Private Home Library Façade
S-00025 Limousine Façade
S-00026 Trophy Wife Façade
S-00027 Trophy Façade (Choose Sport)
S-00028 Happy Family Façade
S-00029 Close Friends Façade
S-00030 Large Downline Façade
S-00031 Customize Your Own Façade

All façades are $39.95 each plus sales tax, shipping and handling. Order any four façades and receive a fifth façade for FREE! Don't Delay, Order Today!

More Façade Line International

It all ends up being about perception and projecting an image, so the Ladies in Façade Line International will want to invest in Façade Line International's Fanny Taye Cosmetic Line (just $9.99 each plus $5 shipping and handling):

S-00032 Irreverent Eye Liner
S-00033 Rude Rouge
S-00034 Monster Mascara (guaranteed to run!)
S-00035 Gutsy Gusher Lip Gloss
S-00036 Sassy Lip Stick
S-00037 Oversized Foundation & Blusher
S-00038 Ceramic Eye Shadow
S-00039 Artificial Tears (adds realism)

For friends and family that have finally fallen off the edge, Façade Line International has a couple of books available to help deprogram devotees from any networking system (only $19.99 plus $5 shipping and handling):

S-00040 *Façade Line International: a Survivor's Guide to Network Marketing and Other MLM (Multi-Level Marketing) Scams.*

S-00041 *Why You Too Should Invest $250 in the Cult of American Free Enterprise.*

Even More Façade Line International

Good health is an important factor for successful emotional and mental balance. That's why we're proud to present Façade Line International's MEGA line of vitamins & health products.

S-00042 Mega-C—Giant sized capsule gives you one (1) month's supply of C in one jumbo-sized dose! Take it once a month and EXPERIENCE the difference! $35.00

S-00043 Mega-Multi—Giant sized capsule gives you one (1) month's supply of all the essential vitamins and minerals in one jumbo-sized dose! Take it once a month and EXPERIENCE the difference! $35.00

S-00044 Mega-Lax—Need a little help being natural? Has nature left you in a bind? Let the choco-express relieve you of any uncertainty. WARNING: this is an extremely FAST-ACTING formula - use only in and around efficient lavatory facilities! Also available as a suppository. $4.99 for 1 chocolate bar

S-00045 Mega-Narexic—Need to lose a few pounds? Take a Mega-Narexic after any meal and feel no guilt. Guaranteed to bring up even the most stubborn of meals. WARNING: this is an extremely FAST-ACTING formula - use only in and around efficient lavatory facilities! $4.99 for 1 chocolate bar

S-00046 Detroit River Juice—Feeling a little blue? Would your rather look green? Finest imported juice from the source. Guaranteed to do something. A little nip every day will do you...! $19.99 for 1 liter

Façade Line
International Tools

If you're truly that desperate to throw away your money, Façade Line International has a complete line of Network Building Support Tools just for you:

Videos $19.99 plus $5 shipping & handling each:

S-00047 *I Bought Success and YOU CAN TOO!*
S-00048 *The Quest and Purchase of Distinction*
S-00049 *Charge It! and Project Abundance!*
S-00050 *I DIDN'T! and YOU CAN TOO!*
S-00051 *Prospects Unaware: How to Get an Unsuspecting Prospect to Believe that He/She Is Coming to a Social Event*

Books $19.99 plus $5 shipping & handling each:

S-00052 *I Bought Success and YOU CAN TOO!*
S-00053 *The Quest and Purchase of Distinction*
S-00054 *Charge It! and Project Abundance!*
S-00055 *I DIDN'T! and YOU CAN TOO!*

S-00056 *Prospects Unaware: How to Get an Unsuspecting Prospect to Believe that He/She Is Coming to a Social Event*

Also available from Façade Line International is the Network Junkies "Must" Collection of Books, Tapes & Videos (just $21.99 each Plus $5 shipping & handling):

S-00057 *Drink and Grow Rich: and Die Fat*
S-00058 *The Magic of Eating Big*
S-00059 *Silly La' Porker's Monkey Book: How to Train Monkeys to be Your Network Marketing Groupies*
S-00060 *Up the MLM or Network*
S-00061 *I Might! (Would You?)*
S-00062 *Cutting Your Own Strings (and Other Appendages)*
S-00063 *How I Raised Myself from Failure to Façade through Illusion*
S-00064 *The Power of Positive Sleeping*
S-00065 *MegaDoubts: Eliminating Negative Friends and Family*
S-00066 *MegaSpends: How to Spend Your Annual Income - or More - on Networking*
S-00067 *The 10? Kernels of Mediocrity*
S-00068 *How to Buy Your Network with Little or No Money Down: Other Zero Cash Financing Techniques and the Secrets of Offshore Credit Cards*
S-00069 *The New Revised Network Marketer's Multi-dialect Dictionary*
- Immediately be able to translate the 16 major North American network marketing and MLM dialects

- You'll never feel out of place again at an "opportunity" meeting again because you'll actually understand what they're saying
- Plus, other useful tips on how to avoid being invited to one
- How to immediately identify if you're being recruited

All of the above books are also available in 8-track and adhesive tape.

Façade Line International, One Last Time...

This brings us to the final product offering from Façade Line International:

S-00070 Gift Certificates—Don't know what to buy that pesky upline of yours for that next gift-giving occasion? Buy gift certificate distributorships for your friends and relatives for their birthdays and other gift-giving occasions online via Façade Line International's web site. $25.00 to $125.00

S-00071 Sham Simple Gift Certificate
(1st level distributor) $25.00
S-00072 Bogus Red Gift Certificate
(2nd level distributor) $50.00
S-00073 Pseudo Bead Gift Certificate
(3rd level distributor) $75.00

S-00074 Cubic Zirconium Gift Certificate
(4th level distributor) $100.00
S-00075 Sham Rock Gift Certificate
(5th level distributor) $125.00
(Super Steal!)

May the façade be with you...

PART IV

INTERNET SITES, BOTH FOR AND AGAINST NETWORK MARKETING

Another Legal Disclaimer: The following list has been compiled over a number of years. The utmost in care has been taken to validate each company and link listed herein. If you feel that a link and/or company that appear on this list should/should not be included in this list, please contact the author via the publisher with written proof demonstrating that the information contained herein is not correct (including the pre-1995 date that your company took over the domain or started the website along with supporting documentation that the site was never used by another company, or you, for network marketing or MLM purposes). If something has been included in this list by error, I apologize in advance and upon proper notice will remove the reference from future copies of the published version of this book. The author, contributors, research team and publisher of this book do not endorse and have not validated any of the content of any of the following Internet sites. It is up to each and every individual to validate the content of each site listed for themselves and cannot hold the author, contributors, research team and/or publisher responsible or liable for any content contained in any of the sites listed in this book. As previously stated, all trade names, trademarks, service marks, etc. mentioned in this section (and throughout the entire book) are the sole property of their owners and their respective companies.

Company and Distributor Sites: the Ones That Have Survived, So Far

1st Family Internet Access
http://www.1stfamily.com/

Abode of the Eternal Tao
http://www.abodetao.com/

Ace Media Promotions
http://www.acemedia.com/

Alliance USA (now called Sportron International)
http://www.csz.com/alliance.html
http://www.healthbiz.net/index.html

Alpine Industries
http://www.alpineindustries.com/

Alternative Income Strategies
http://www.second-income.com/

America Works
http://www.americaworks.net/

American Communications Network
http://www.acninc.com/

American Pro Se Association
http://www.legalhelp.org/

Amway (Alticor, Access Business Group, Quixtar and
Pyxis Innovations)
http://www.amway.com/
http://www.alticor.com/companies/companies.html
http://www.alticor.com/companies/access_bus_group.html
http://www.quixtar.com/
http://www.alticor.com/news/faq.html

AquaSource
http://www.aquasource.uk.co/

Avon
http://www.avon.com/

Awareness Corporation
http://www.awarecorp.com/live/home/

Biometics International
http://www.biometics.com/

BodyWise International, Inc.
http://www.bodywise.com/

Bountiful Bust Cream (now Noni Juice, etc.)
http://www.pathcom.com/~ianw/bount.htm

Cabouchon
http://www.cabouchon.com/

Cashexpress
http://cashexpress.net/

Cell Tech
http://www.celltech.com/

Changes International
http://www.changesinternational.com/

Charmelle
http://www.charmelle.com

Calorad
http://www.calorad2000.com/

Coupon Connection of America
http://www.ccoa.com

Dare To Succeed
http://www.dreamwater.org/biz/ibd/

DiRon Marketing
http://www.diron.com/

Discovery Toys
http://www.discoverytoysinc.com/

Duplicator
http://www.theduplicator.com/

Empower Net
http://www.empowernet.com/

Endless Vacation Trust
http://www.flash.net/~evt/

Enrich International (now Unicity Network)
http://www.enrich.com/

Entrepreneur's CyberShop
http://www.bossbiz.com/

E'OLA
http://www.eola.com/

Excel Communications, Inc.
http://www.excel.com/us/index.html

Fat B Gone (Doctors only direct sales)
http://www.nutritiondynamics.com/fatbgone/

Financial Independence Network
http://www.debtfree.com/

Forever Living Products
http://www.foreverliving.com/

For Mor International
http://www.formorintl.com/company.html

Freedomstarr Communications
http://www.webpost.net/em/Employment/HomePage.html

Fuller Brush Company
http://www.fuller.com/

Grace Cosmetics (now Pro-Ma Systems International)
http://www.gracecosmetics.com/

Health Technologies Network
http://www.moneytalks.com/

HealthWise Solutions (now Transfer Factor)
http://www.wise1.com/

Herbalife (**note**: Mark Hughes, the founder of Herbalife,
died of cancer in May 2000 at the young age of 44 years
old — guess the herbs didn't work so well for him!)
http://www.herbalife.com/

Horizons Marketing Group, Inc
http://www.horizons-marketing.com/

ISI Value Network
http://www.mrbo.com

Jafra
http://www.jafra.com/intro.html

Kaire International
http://www.kaire.com/

Karemor International, Inc. (now VitaMist Oral Spray
Vitamins)
http://www.karemor.com/
http://www.vitamist.com

KingsWay
http://www.kingsway-global.com/

Kleeneze
http://www.trevor-kleeneze.com/

Lametco International
http://www.lametcointl.com/

Leaders Club
http://www.leadersclub.com/

Life Extension International Inc.
http://www.lef.org/

Life Plus
http://www.lifeplus.com/

Lifestyles International World headquarters
http://www.lifestyles-mlm.com/

Longevity Network
http://www.longevitynetwork.com/

Mannatech Inc.
http://www.mannatech.com/

Market America
http://www.marketamerica.com/

Mary Kay
http://www.marykay.com/

Matol
http://www.matol.com/

Maxxis 2000 (example of a company that has used, in the past, religion a as reason to join)
http://www.maxxis2000.com/

Melaleuca
http://www.melaleuca.com/

Morinda Inc. (Tahitian Noni juice)
http://www.morinda.com/

Multi-Level Classifieds - The Zone
http://worldentre.com/thezone.htm

Multi-Pure
http://www.multipureco.com/

N/A/T/O International
http://www.natoint.com/p1.asp

Nature's Sunshine
http://www.naturessunshine.com/

Network Marketing News (now called MLM Pro)
http://www.mlmpro.com/index.html
http://www.mlmpro.com/index.html

Neways
http://www.neways.com/

New Image International
http://www.newimageint.com/

New Vision International
http://www.new-vision-intl.com/

Nikken Industries
http://www.nikken.com/

Noevir U.S.A., Inc
http://www.noevirusa.com/

NuSkin International
http://www.nuskin.com/

Nutrition For Life International
http://www.nutritionforlife.com/

Oxyfresh
http://www.oxyfresh.com/

Oxygen for Life
http://www.oxygenforlife.co.za/

Pinnacle Nutrition International (now New Vision
International, see above)
http://pinnaclenutrition.com/

Pre-Paid Legal Services, Inc.
http://www.pplsi.com/

Primerica Financial Services
http://ww3.primerica.com/public/
They have a beautiful chart that clearly illustrates how few people can actually make a living in network marketing their product. See link at:
http://ww3.primerica.com/public/what/opp/track_record.html
Out of 100,000 distributors, just over 4% make more than $50,000 per year.

Prosper International Limited
http://www.pill.net/

Pro Star International
http://www.prostarnutrition.com/

ProSTEP Inc.
http://www.prostepinc.com/

Quorum International
http://home.pacific.net.hk/~gng/quorum.html

R-Garden
http://www.rgarden.com/

Reliv International
http://www.reliv.com/

Rexall Showcase International (now part of Unicity, see Enrich above)
http://www.rexallshowcase.com/

Royal BodyCare Inc.
http://www.rbcglobenet.com/

Shaklee
http://www.shaklee.com/

Shaperite Concepts, Ltd. (recently merged with 4-Life)
http://www.shaperite.com/
http://www.4-life.com/

Sportron
http://www.sportron.com/

Success-Teams Marketing Support
http://www.successteams.com/

Superb Marketing and Consulting, Inc.
http://www.superbnet.com/

Tel-A-Nation, Inc.
http://www.tel-a-nation.com/

TEL3
http://www.tel3.com/

Tupperware
http://www.tupperware.com/

USANA
http://www.usanainc.com/

U.S. Mortgage Reduction, Inc.
http://www.usmr.com/

Vaxa International
http://vaxa.com/

Viva America
http://www.vivalife.com/index.htm

Watkins
http://www.watkinsonline.com/default.cfm

Wellness International Network, Ltd
http://www.winltd.com/

World-Link, Inc.
http://www.world-link.net/

Your Opportunity Page
http://www.geocities.com/WallStreet/4016/

The Graveyard: Network Marketing Internet Sites That Have Died

The following sites are no longer available since the original research was conducted in 1995

Distributor and Company Sites Graveyard, May They "Rest in Peace" (R.I.P.)

R.I.P. ABW Enterprises
http://www.abw642.com/index.htm

R.I.P. Achievers Unlimited
http://www.primenet.com/~keven

R.I.P. AdNet Online
http://www.adnetonline.com

R.I.P. Advanced Business Builders
http://www.purevision.com/abb/

R.I.P. Advanced Research Concepts, Inc
http://www.arcltd.com/

R.I.P. Advantage Marketing Systems
http://WWW.AMOSONLINE.Com

R.I.P. AdverWorld (bankrupt, but still online)
http://www.AdverWorld.com/

R.I.P. AdNet Online
http://www.adnetonline.com/

R.I.P. Ad-Venture 2000
http://www.ad-venture2000.com/

R.I.P. Alive International
http://www.em-co.com/mco/alive/alive.html

R.I.P. America's Team Nutrition
http://www.americas-team.com/

R.I.P. American Dream
http://www.jim-watkins.com/

R.I.P. American Dream Network
http://www.munymaker.com

R.I.P. American Freeway100
http://www.fw100.com/

R.I.P. Appaloosa
http://www.liberty.com/home/appaloosa/busn.htm

R.I.P. Art of Better Living
http://www.artofbetterliving.com/

R.I.P. Art Partners (domain for sale)
http://www.artpartners.com/

R.I.P. Attainment Mall
http://www.attainment.com/index.htm

R.I.P. ArthroVite
http://www.btinternet.com/~creative/arthrovite/index.html

R.I.P. ATA Publications
http://www.homebizopportunities.com/atapublications/

R.I.P. Automated Direct Data System
http://www.earnfromhome.com/

R.I.P. Bayside Internet Services
http://www.bayside.hostings.com/

R.I.P. Best Choice International L.L.C. (domain for sale)
http://www.best-choice.com/

R.I.P. Beverly's Most Powerful Page
http://www.vornet.com/~powerful/

R.I.P. Bi-Tron (no longer MLM)
http://www.liquid-gold.org/

R.I.P. Body & Mind Enterprises
http://members.aol.com/adamdekort/bm_home.htm

R.I.P. Body Electric (domain for sale)
http://www.bodyelec.com/

R.I.P. Body Systems Technology,Inc. (domain for sale)
http://www.bodysystem.com/

R.I.P. Boston-Finney
http://www.electricsavings.com/

R.I.P. Business Builders Club
http://paula.net/bbc/

R.I.P. Business Opportunity
http://www.pond.com/novello/

R.I.P. Business Success Unlimited Inc.
http://www.successunlimited.com

R.I.P. Candlelight Press (domain for sale)
http://www.swswsw.com/
http://www.pma-online.org/scripts/showmember.cfm?code=482

R.I.P. Celestine Health, Inc.
http://www.osteoarthritis.com/

R.I.P. Commission Direct. LTD.
http://www.commissiondirect.com/

R.I.P. Compu-Ed
http://www.compued.com

R.I.P. Consumer Power Unlimited
http://www.vpp.com/cnc

R.I.P. Coupon Savers
http://virtual.phoenix.net/~money/

R.I.P. CyberAdvertising Agency Services
http://www.cyberpages.com/db/company&1&236

R.I.P. DEBTbusters International
http://www.debtbusters.net/

R.I.P. Delfin Systems of Wisdom
http://www.lloyd.com/~bjrsales/

R.I.P. DFW Metro Marketing
http://rampages.onramp.net/~metro/

R.I.P. Dial-1 Communications, Inc.
http://www.dial-1.com/

R.I.P. Diamond Life International
http://www.diamond-life.com

R.I.P. Digital Direct Marketing Group
http://ddmg.com/future/net221.htm

R.I.P. Direct Access Network
http://www.alohanevada.com

R.I.P. Diversified Marketing Concepts
http://dmconcepts.com/

R.I.P. DLC Marketing, Inc. (domain for sale)
http://www.dlcmarketing.com/

R.I.P. Docsweb (domain for sale)
http://www.docsweb.com/

R.I.P. Downline USA
http://www.downlineusa.com

R.I.P. Dynasty Group
http://register.com/dynasty/

R.I.P. Earth Legacy, Inc. (domain for sale)
http://earthlegacy.com/

R.I.P. EON 2000
http://www.io.com/~kipstips/EON/1279.htm

R.I.P. Equinox International (bankrupt!)
http://www.equinoxinternational.com/

R.I.P. Equity Accelerator
http://www.ultranet.com/~hixdave/Accel.html

R.I.P. Espial (no longer MLM)
http://www.espial.com/

R.I.P. Essential Express Health Industries
http://www.caloradnet.bc.ca/

R.I.P. Essential Oils
http://www.redbay.com/oils/

R.I.P. Filler Up
http://www.fillerup.com

R.I.P. Financial Freedom
http://www.ilmenterprises.idsite.com/

R.I.P. Fortuna Alliance (FTC stepped-in and shut them down!)
http://www.ultranet.com/~success1/fa.html

R.I.P. Fox Telcom Inc.
http://www.world1team.com/

R.I.P. FreeLife International
http://www.freelifeonline.com/

R.I.P. FreeNet
http://multi-level.com/freenet

R.I.P. Free Yellow Pages (no longer MLM)
http://www.freeyellow.com/

R.I.P. Future Net
http://futurenet-online.com

R.I.P. Genesis 2000 (no longer MLM)
http://www.genesis2000.com/

R.I.P. Global Entrepreneurs Network - GEN
Website is now Global Education Network (no longer MLM)
http://www.gen.com/

R.I.P. Global Marketing Group
http://www.g-m-g.com

R.I.P. Global Success Builders
http://www.link.ca/~success/

R.I.P. Global Ventures (no longer MLM)
http://www.global-ventures.com/

R.I.P. Global Wellness Club
http://www.globalwellnessclub.com/

R.I.P. Globaltron Systems
http://www.globaltron.com/

R.I.P. G.M.Enterprises
http://www.redbay.com/gme/

R.I.P. Golf Concepts
http://gamemasters.netpath.net/

R.I.P. Gourmet Club
http://alaph.com/

R.I.P. Great News International
http://www.gnint.com/

R.I.P. Great Sex in a Bottle
http://adpages.com/usa2/greatsex.htm

R.I.P. Grocery Club
http://members.aol.com/AngelHamm/index.html

R.I.P. Growth Advantage, The
http://www.tgadvantage.com/

R.I.P. Guard-A-Child
http://www.guard-a-child.com

R.I.P. Healing Network
http://www.gen.com/healingnet/research.htm

R.I.P. Health Club Network
http://www.healthclubnetwork.com/

R.I.P. Health Dynamics Research Co.
http://hdrc.com/

R.I.P. Herbal Healthcare Alternatives
http://www.valley-internet.com/~jsturgis/index.htm

R.I.P. High Opportunity Petroleum Enterprises Inc.
http://www.hopeinc.com/

R.I.P. Higher Ideals (domain for sale)
http://www.higherideals.com/

R.I.P. Home Beauty Apparatus
http://www.healthhomedevice.com/beauty.html

R.I.P. House of Lloyd Income Opportunities (bankrupt)
http://www.whiterose.net/catw/index.htm

R.I.P. I.D.E.A. Concepts
http://www.ideaconcepts.com/

R.I.P. Incredible Products
http://www.incredibleproducts.com/

R.I.P. Inside Network
http://www.best.com/~fin/inside.htm

R.I.P. Inspire Magazine
http://www.inspiremagazine.com

R.I.P. Intermatrix Golden Distributors, Ltd.
http://www.imgltd.com/

R.I.P. International Association for Network Marketing
http://yi.com/ianm/index.php

R.I.P. International Heritage, Inc
http://www.aable.com/ihi

R.I.P. International Marketer's Group
http://www2.spidernet.net/web/~marwan/img/img3.html

R.I.P. Investors International
http://www.cyberius.com/investors/

R.I.P. JC&C Investors International
http://www.jc-c.com/

R.I.P. Jeff Campbell's HomeLife Systems (no longer MLM)
http://www.jeffcampbell.com/

R.I.P. Jewelway International
http://www.jewelway.com/

R.I.P. Journey Telecom
http://www.journeytelecard.com/

R.I.P. Ketch-up
http://www.ketch-up.com/

R.I.P. K*I*D*S Shield Child Protection System
http://www.dogonnet.com/kids/

R.I.P. K.R.V. Internet Consulting
http://members.tripod.com/~KVento/krv.htm

R.I.P. Leadership Dynamics Institute
http://www.leadership-dynamics.com/aboutild.htm

R.I.P. Learn to Earn
http://home.earthlink.net/~drdln/

R.I.P. Liberty Gold International
http://www.u-net.com/liberty

R.I.P. Life Force
http://www.readysoft.es/lifeplus/lifeforce/lfindex.html

R.I.P. Life's Majyk
http://members.aol.com/lifesmajyk/health.htm

R.I.P. Lifefoods
http://www.lifefoods.com/

R.I.P. LifeTrends International (no longer MLM)
http://www.lifetrendsintl.com/index.asp

R.I.P. LifeZest Unlimited
http://lifezest.com/

R.I.P. Light Force
http://www.lightforcedis.com/

R.I.P. Links Direct (domain for sale)
http://www.linksdirect.com/

R.I.P. list.mktplace.net
http://www.mktplace.net/things/list/

R.I.P. Lose Weight and Earn Money
http://www.concentric.net/~jrichter/

R.I.P. MB Enterprises
http://www.mbent.com

R.I.P. Maddy Nutrition Corporation
http://www.maddy.com/

R.I.P. Mail-Link (no longer MLM)
http://www.mail-link.com/

R.I.P. MagNet Telecom Inc. (no longer MLM)
http://www.magnetcom.com/

R.I.P. Making Money
http://pages.prodigy.com/MI/knemchak/knemchak2.html

R.I.P. Marine Minerals (no longer MLM)
http://www.marineminerals.com/

R.I.P. Marketing Network Company
http://www.marknetwork.com/

R.I.P. Martel Enterprises
http://www.globalpac.com/martal/main3.htm

R.I.P. MegaNet
http://www.meganets.org/

R.I.P. MLMSchool
http://www.mlmschool.com/

R.I.P. MLSA
http://mlsacomline.com/

R.I.P. Money Making Computer Program
http://homepages.ihug.co.nz/~owenp/

R.I.P. Natural Connections, Inc.
http://www.naturalconnections.com/

R.I.P. Natural Health
http://www.inetme.com/iom/team/n-health.html

R.I.P. Natural efx
http://www.naturalefx.com/

R.I.P. Natural Resource (domain for sale)
http://www.naturalresource.com/

R.I.P. Naturesbest (no longer MLM)
http://www.naturesbest.com/

R.I.P. Nature's Own
http://www.naturesown.com.au/

R.I.P. NeTel
http://www.netel.net/

R.I.P. NetOpp - The Internet Opportunity
http://www.netopp.com/

R.I.P. NetSafe
http://www.netsafe.com/

R.I.P. Netway Marketing
http://www.perfectway.com

R.I.P. New Generation Marketing
http://www.binarygoldmine.com/

R.I.P. Nu-Tegrity Network
http://www.nutegrity.com/

R.I.P. NutriCare (no longer MLM)
http://nutricare.com/

R.I.P. Nutriplus
http://www.nutriplus.com/

R.I.P. Omega Communications, LLC
http://www.voyageronline.net/~omega/

R.I.P. ONeLINERS
http://www.hiwaay.net/ONeLINERS/index.html

R.I.P. Opportunity Now
http://www.opportunitynow.com/

R.I.P. Pacific Network Marketing Group
http://www.aa.net/pacific.nw.marketing/

R.I.P. Pangea
http://www.multilevellink.com/pangea.html

R.I.P. PCMartin, Inc.
http://www.pcmartin.com/Welcome.shtml

R.I.P. Personal Wealth Systems, Inc.
http://krel.iea.com/pws/index.html

R.I.P. Pilex (no longer MLM)
http://www.hemorrhoid.com/

R.I.P. P.I.L.L.
http://www.cashflow.com/pill.htm

R.I.P. P.M./Life Tronix
http://207.158.226.190/index.htm

R.I.P. PowerPage
http://www.powerpageinc.com/

R.I.P. Pre-built Downline
http://www.macor.com/%20d/2547

R.I.P. Premiere Permanent Downline
http://www.ppdweb.com/

R.I.P. PrimeQuest
http://www.primequest.com/

R.I.P. Progressive Fortune
http://www.web4ads.com/fortunes/MH81621/

R.I.P. Promotions 2000
http://www.promo2000.com/index.html

R.I.P. Prosper International League
http://www.clicklink.com/prosper/now.html

R.I.P. Power Ad
http://spring-board.com/123ez/rozco/

R.I.P. Race Base
http://www.racebase.com/

R.I.P. RealNet Marketing Group
http://www.rnmg.com/

R.I.P. Real Vision
http://www.angelfire.com/ky/RealVision/index.html

R.I.P. Restores
http://www.sacbiz.com/restores/

R.I.P. R + M Watson Company
http://www.r-mwatson.com/

R.I.P. Roberts Evergreen Products Ltd
http://www.immunohelp.com/demo/company.htm

R.I.P. Secret of The World's Oldest Man
http://www.coral-way.com/html/Secrets.htm

R.I.P. Service Express
http://www.barefoot.com/service/

R.I.P. Simplicity (domain for sale)
http://successpages.com/simplicity.html

R.I.P. Simply CD
http://members.aol.com/mrdemitri/scd/index.htm

R.I.P. Soaring Eagle Ventures
http://sportstoddy.com/

R.I.P. SPI'S Mercosul Business Center
http://spi.com.br/~spi/

R.I.P. Starfire International
http://www.star-base.net/

R.I.P. StarQuest Corporation
http://www.dreambig.com/

R.I.P. StarTronix
http://www.startronix.com/

R.I.P. StarWatch Marketing
http://www.ntplx.net/~starwtch/business_opportunity.html

R.I.P. STEF International
http://www.stef.com/

R.I.P. Streamline International
http://www.ftc.gov/opa/2001/06/streamline.htm

R.I.P. SuperPage Systems, Inc.
http://www.pagersusa.com/

R.I.P. SupremeHealth
http://www.supremehealth.com/

R.I.P. Sweet Savings
http://www.sweetsavings.com/

R.I.P. Sweet Success Nutritional Products (sadly, this site now belongs to the Syrian Social Nationalist Party)
http://www.ssnp.com/

R.I.P. Symmetry Corporation
http://www.symmetrynet.com/

R.I.P. Team One International (no longer MLM)
http://www.teamone.com.sg/
-or- http://web.singnet.com.sg/~teamone/

R.I.P. TeamUp International, Inc.
http://www.wp.com/teamup/

R.I.P. The Network
http://rainbow.rmi.net/~ntwork/

R.I.P. The Security Council
http://virtual-adnet.com/therock/secure/secur46.htm

R.I.P. The Waters Edge
http://www.escape.ca/~dwaters/

R.I.P. TNA Power Team
http://www.tnacyberteam.com/

R.I.P. Total Success Solutions, Inc.
http://magnet.mwci.net/mall/relonet/tssi/

R.I.P. TPN - The Peoples Network (domain for sale)
http://www.thepeoplesnetwork.com/

R.I.P. TradeNet Marketing, Inc.
http://www.tradenetmarketing.com/

R.I.P. Trendmark International
http://www.american-shoppers.com/

R.I.P. Trim Team
http://www.trimteam.com/

R.I.P. True Health Inc.
http://afcomm.com/true_health/

R.I.P. TruHealth
http://www.biz.net/truhealth/

R.I.P. Trushnet
http://www.trushnet.com/

R.I.P. Unified Worldwide
http://www.ipinc.net/~intmedia/

R.I.P. United Charities Assistance Network
http://www.icenter.net/~philliph/

R.I.P. Universal Pre-Paid Fuel Card
http://www.geocities.com/Eureka/Park/4416/

R.I.P. United Prosper Club
http://www.aa.net/pacific.nw.marketing/united.html

R.I.P. Value Net Incorporated (domain for sale)
http://www.valuenetinc.com/

R.I.P. Viewpoint Success Group
http://www.vpp.com/vsg/index.html

R.I.P. Vision Quest International
http://www.bsuccessful.com/

R.I.P. Vitality Unlimited
http://www.pamall.com/01na.html

R.I.P. Vitall
http://www.sonnet.co.uk/fry-int/mlm.htm

R.I.P. Vitamist
http://colorado.nbci.net/Vitamins/

R.I.P. Voyager
http://www.voyagerusa-brazil.com

R.I.P. Wealth International
http://www.crystalcanyon.com/wealth

R.I.P. Wealthcom
http://www.multilevellink.com/wealth.html

R.I.P. Whealth
http://www.swalson.com/cdm/

R.I.P. World Class Network
http://www.wcnetwork.com/

R.I.P. WorldConnect Communications, Inc.
http://www.worldconnectcomm.com/

R.I.P. World Trading Company (domain for sale)
http://www.1wtc.com/

R.I.P. Worldwide Merchandise
http://www.worldwidemerchandise.com/

R.I.P. WorldWide Opportunities Network (domain for sale)
http://www.wwon.com/

R.I.P. WOW! Entertainment
http://wownetwork.com/

R.I.P. Yorkbest Total Marketing
http://www.hk.super.net/~gng/ybhome.html

R.I.P. Young Living Essential Oils (no longer MLM)
http://www.essentialsolutions.com/

Debate Sites Graveyard

R.I.P. http://www.multi-level.com/
R.I.P. http://www.lycos.com/wguide/wire/wire_484445_
47604_3_61.html

R.I.P. This page used to be in Asia somewhere...
http://myhome.hananet.net/~try77kr/link.htm

R.I.P. Amway Corporation and High-Level Amway
Distributors Sued
http://www.riaa.com/antipir/releases/amway.htm

R.I.P. Amway: Facts for Thought (was last a site about cats)
http://www.skyenet.net/~jackie/

R.I.P. Amway: Fact OR Fiction?
http://www.ezonline.com/eagle01

R.I.P. Amway Motivational Organizations: The Nightmare
Builders
http://www.tc.umn.edu/nlhome/m307/wilke001/amway.html

R.I.P. Amway related links...
http://www.willynet.com/rglasser/amway/amlinks.html

R.I.P. Amway Speaks: Memorable Quotes
http://www.rickross.com/reference2/amway10.html

R.I.P. Amway: The Untold Story (see Mirror Site)
http://www.teleport.com/%7Eschwartz

R.I.P. Amway: The Untold Story: American Journal
http://www.rickross.com/reference2/amway5.html

R.I.P. Amway: The Untold Story: Directly Speaking
http://home.onestop.net/nomorescam/schwartz/directly.htm

R.I.P. Amway: The Untold Story: Hayden Lawsuit
http://home.onestop.net/nomorescam/schwartz/hayden.htm

R.I.P. Amway: The Untold Story: Hanrahan Lawsuit
http://www.rickross.com/reference2/amway6.html

R.I.P. Amway: The Untold Story: Quotables
http://home.onestop.net/nomorescam/schwartz/quotes.htm

R.I.P. An Equinox expose site
http://www.knoxtoo.com/printer/enox.htm

R.I.P. Better Business Bureaus Scam Alerts and informa-

tion on multilevel marketing
http://www.hbn-intelinet.com/bbb.htm

R.I.P. Forbes: Million-man sales force
http://207.87.27.10/forbes/97/0324/5906063a.htm

R.I.P. FTC surf day (500 COMPANIES)
http://www.ftc.gov/opa/9612/surf.htm

R.I.P. FTC tips to avoid pyramid schemes
http://www.ftc.gov/pyramid/index.htm

R.I.P. Herbalife Lawsuit Web Site
http://herbalawsuit.com/

R.I.P. Herbalife complaints and litigation
http://www.herbalawsuit.com/hpage.htm

R.I.P. High Level Equinox Representative Tells All!!!
http://www.knoxtoo.com/printer/truth.htm

R.I.P. Laundry CD
http://www.dvmay.com/lcd/

R.I.P. Lawsuit against Herbalife
http://www.herbalawsuit.com/

R.I.P. MLM Insider's worst companies
http://www.mlminsider.com/worst.html

R.I.P. My Equinox Independent Distributor Bad
Experience
http://www.knoxtoo.com/printer/enox.htm

R.I.P. Natural World

http://www.naturalworld.com/

R.I.P. Nightmare Builders
http://www.tc.umn.edu/nlhome/m307/wilke001/amway.html

R.I.P. Response To The Anti-Amway Site
http://www.flash.net/~probandt/response/

R.I.P. The Other Side of the Plan
http://members.iclub.org/dcmdg/

R.I.P. Wall Street Journal: Bitter Herb Distributor Hopes
Web Site Can Remedy Situation
http://www.herbalawsuit.com/wallst.htm

R.I.P. Generic Overview of the MLM Industry
http://home1.gte.net/drrn19/index.htm

But the Real Debate Lives On at These Sites

Amway: An Insider's Perspective
http://www-acc.scu.edu/~jgreenfield/amway_home.html

Amway or Scamway? (you might have to navigate through the site to get to the article)
http://caic.org.au/zcommerc.htm

Amway: The Untold Story – Mirror Site
http://www.suburbia.com.au/~fun/amway/

Better Business Bureau
http://www.bbb.org/

Cagey Consumer
http://www.geocities.com/WallStreet/5395/consumer.html

Equinox Exposed by National Media
http://www.metroactive.com/papers/metro/10.03.96/cover/multilevel-9640.html

Equinox sued by former distributors
http://www.metroactive.com/papers/metro/11.14.96/mlm-update-9646.html

Equinox found guilty of lying
http://www.wa.gov/ago/releases/rel_marketing_081596.html

Equinox: Pyramid scam makes inroads under our own eyes
http://www.illinimedia.com/di/archives/1997/September/19/p13_priestcol.html

FTC – MLM document
http://www.ftc.gov/bcp/conline/pubs/invest/mlm.htm

J. Hubert Funk's Scam-O-Rama
http://members.aol.com/drcryptic/scamorama.htm

Multi-Level Marketing
http://www.usps.gov/websites/depart/inspect/pyramid.htm

National Fraud Information Center
http://www.fraud.org

Networking Multi-Level Trap
http://student.uq.edu.au/~py101663/miscult/commerc.htm

Other Side Of The Plan
http://www.getfacts.com/amway/tosotp/tosotp.html

Perils of Amway
http://www.apollowebworks.com/amway/

pyramid scams
http://www.ftc.gov/opa/1999/9912/cops2.htm

Shaking the Money Tree
http://www.metroactive.com/papers/metro/10.03.96/cover/multilevel-9640.html

Steve, George and Dave's Amway Page
http://www.encomix.es/~duoduo/am_otros.htm

The MLM Survivors Website
http://www.mlmsurvivor.com/survivor1.htm

The power of positive inspiration - by Paul Klebniov
http://skepdic.com/klebniov.html

The Skeptic's Dictionary - "Amway"
http://skepdic.com/amway.html

The things they will say to profit from your dreams
http://www.angelfire.com/or/amwaydreamers/

Truth About Multi-level Marketing Programs
http://www.insiderreports.com/bizrprts/b2514.htm

What's Wrong With Multi-Level Marketing?
http://www.vandruff.com/mlm.html

Some Additional Searchable Sites, Magazines and Articles

http://www.multilevel.com/

http://www.multi-level-marketing.com/

http://www.bestmall.com/mall/mlmypnam.htm

http://www.webfanatix.com/network_marketing_general_compan.htm

http://www.netegories.com/usa/m-links/multi_level_marketing_usa.htm

http://www.keyworlds.com/n/network_marketing_health.htm

MLM.com
http://www.mlm.com/

Money Maker's Monthly
http://www.mmmonthly.com/

Cashflow.com
http://www.cashflow.com/usatel.htm

MLM Watchdog
http://www.mlmwatchdog.com/

Entrepreneur Magazine article
http://www.entrepreneur.com/Magazines/Copy_of_MA_Se
gArticle/0,4453,297774,00.html

For Those that Still Use Newsgroups (Usenet)

Note: Since I haven't used Usenet in years, there is a strong chance that these boards may no longer be active — if you subscribe to any newsgroups, then you'll want to search on standard MLM or network marketing terms to find corresponding boards to this list. Happy hunting.

alt.business.multi-level
alt.business.multi-level.exceltel
alt.business.multi-level.moderated
alt.business.multi-level.scam
alt.business.multi-level.scam.scam.scam
alt.business.multi-level.watkins
alt.recover.mlm

PART V

SPECIAL BONUS SECTION

One Last Legal Disclaimer: The following bonus section is allegedly the original text of Philip Kern's book *Fake It Till You Make It.* A search of the US Copyright Office database disclosed Mr. Kerns other copyright on the book about Jonesville and that cult, but for whatever reason, Mr. Kerns chose not to take out an official copyright on his book *Fake It Till You Make It* and it is therefore part of the public domain. For the first time in two decades, it is once again available as a special bonus to my readers.

Fake It Till You Make It

by Philip Kerns
published in 1982

Dedicated to Victoria,
who has always been an inspiration in my life

Introduction

This incredible story is true. These pages unfold well-guarded secrets of Amway Corporation's "Winner's Circle." It is an account of over one million distributors, many of whom are considered to be carbon copies of the corporation's curators, Jay VanAndel and Rich DeVos. The sheer numbers of this group draw politicians like Ronald Reagan, Gerald Ford and Jesse Helms. This massive worldwide corporation has over the years become a haven for professional singers and motion picture stars. It has not been uncommon for pastors, evangelists and gospel singers to trade their humble flocks for sheep of a different kind.

Amway has been frequently called a "rags to riches" corporation, which was pulled up by its bootstraps in 1959 and now in 1982 proudly exceeds the $1.4 billion mark in retail sales. Although impressions of the mechanics of the company will be described from time to time, the focal point of the story is directed towards the distributors themselves and the Amway Distributors Association of America, a separate non-profit entity. The issue in this book is not the Corporation and not SOAP, but rather distributors who have a mission and a hope, a dream. Their mission is to sponsor others and their hope and dream is to build a financial empire. To many of the distributors, no price is too great to pay in order to achieve this mission and this dream. One will discover in reading through these pages that there is indeed, a price to be paid—to a "hidden" business carefully concealed behind the infrastructure of Amway's hierarchy. It is a multi-million dollar enterprise, cleverly designed and fueled by excitement and hero worship.

Some have said that this "ghost" system of "non-Amway" produced materials has created a massive surge of grabby avariciousness from many of the top leaders, much more today than ever before. Other distributors complain that this selfishness is destroying the credibility of their own businesses, and they feel that if this display of outlandish coveting continues, it may inevitably destroy their own personal enterprises.

The complaints I have heard are endless. They include everything from outright lying to prospective distributors to even exalting leaders as prophets of God. I have compiled reams of information and interviewed hundreds of distributors all across the nation and abroad concerning Amway's distributor organization.

This story would not have been possible without the courageous and outspoken contributions made by people in Amway, some of whom are mentioned within the pages of this book. Some of these individuals, today, are still Amway distributors operating successful businesses! They have vehemently protested the cult-like tactics used by certain leaders in Amway. In their official complaints, they have cited harassment, character assassination and religious fanaticism—all of these tactics used to peddle huge volumes of products not related to Amway.

This book also contains my own personal experiences in the Amway business. Included is my association and subsequent recruitment by two of Amway's most highly acclaimed distributors. The names of these distributors and others have been concealed.

Places and characteristics also have been changed. If you see names of famous persons you recognize, it is because they are peripheral and not key in nature. My full intention in writing this book is not to tear down but rather to help open the eyes of many persons who are being deceived.

Therefore, I believe it is justifiable to say that this is not a "classic mudraker." Instead it is two years of carefully documented affidavits, letters, notes and tape recordings uncovering this mysterious and very lucrative "ghost" system within Amway's legitimate enterprise.

In Amway's own Corporate Compendium an unusual question is asked in bold italics, "is Amway a Religious or Political Cult?" Never before have I seen such a question in any corporate literature. Could it be that they too, are beginning to feel the stress of a distributorship organization out of control, thereby possibly apologizing for the actions of those within its very own ranks?

This is mystery. It was designed to be a valuable spiritual handbook to assist you in making a more objective decision—whether you are already in the ranks or considering subscription to this organization.

Phil Kerns

CHAPTER 1

The Dream

The year 1981 was a time of fury. Our nation was staggered by the shooting of President Reagan, and the entire world cringed when Pope John Paul II was gunned down in Rome. Millions of Americans watched from the protection of their living rooms as hails of bullets smashed through Anwar Sadat's reviewing stand. It was a bitter year of turmoil for Poland, El Salvador and the Middle East. West Europeans marched for peace as Libya's Muammar Kaddafi terrorized the world with his threats.

Somehow through all of the pandemonium in the world, pomp still proved to be glorious when Prince Charles and Lady Diana exchanged their wedding vows. Millions watched with childlike fascination as this procession of royalty fulfilled this once glorious nation's traditional dream.

Another event of international prominence to catch the attention of the public's eye was the dedication of the magnificently restored Amway Grand Plaza Hotel in Grand Rapids, Michigan. The registration list for this gala event revealed 600 prominent guests. Some of the most notable persons to be invited included President and Mrs. Ronald Reagan, former President and Mrs. Gerald R. Ford, Vice President and Mrs. George Bush, President Jose Portillo of

Mexico, Prime Minister Pierre Trudeau of Canada, former President Valery Gisgard d'Estaing of France, Foreign Minister Sunao Sonada of Japan and Hollywood's acclaimed Bob Hope.

It was a grand affair of elegance and nobility. During the early evening hours on the night of the dedication, security officers directed traffic for dozens of limousines, each struggling for a place in which to deposit its distinguished guests. It was an exquisite parade of the elite and well-to-do. Each was being escorted into this newly renovated building which was previously known as the Old Pantlind Hotel. Inside the scene was breathtaking. The vaulted ceilings gleamed with approximately one million square inches of hand applied gold leaf. Richly polished mahogany paneling provided resonance for the newly painted decor. Prisms of light shot about the expansive rooms, bouncing from one luxuriant chandelier to another. Bouquets of fragrantly scented flowers added an aroma of paradise to the surroundings.

This event would be historically noted as a week of splendor never to be forgotten. Here under one roof had gathered many of the world's most well heeled and opulent leaders. All of this international socializing would not have been possible without a "Dream." This "Dream" began in the minds and hearts of Amway's founders, Rich DeVos and Jay VanAndel. The entire vision was the product of two determined entrepreneurs. They had built an empire, and it was now time to enjoy the prestige and fruits of their labors.

In looking across the expanses of the world, millions of determined entrepreneurs can be found. They may be seen pushing a sandwich cart in New York or even selling ash from the eruption of Mt. St. Helens. Determination and creativity are the two vital ingredients necessary to propel these daring and ambitious tradesmen on towards success.

Each has probably chosen to ignore the circumstances, which constantly surround and threaten him with extinction.

Usually his pride or bravado catapults him beyond all obstacles, thus proving to all unbelievers that he is, in fact, a doer! All scoffers are put to open shame by his ability to achieve, and excel.

Of course, no tall businessmen will produce with the same degree of vigor and enthusiasm. Some look to the trade as a mere livelihood, while others see the market place as a very competitive battleground where there can only be "winners" and "losers." The Amway distributor, like many other entrepreneurs, has much determination. However, uniquely apart from most other businesses, this business requires little "creativity." "That's the beauty of the business," some distributors will tell others. All the groundwork has all ready been laid. One only has to remember four things: Setup a meeting, go to a meeting, recruit someone at the meeting and set up another meeting. It is as simple as that!

Or is it? After several months in the business, I found that it was not as easy as I had been led to believe. In fact, there was a price, which I personally had to pay when selling the "Dream." This price was less time with my family and a deficit in my checking account!

After leaving Amway myself and during the course of my investigation into the very depths of this company, I met Michelle. She is an attractive young blonde who works for a very active inner city Christian ministry in Portland, Oregon.

She explained to me how she had been approached about Amway by Larry, a close friend whom she had known for several years. One day at work Larry came by. Michelle was shocked to see him wearing a suit. "He never wears a suit, not even to church!" she thought to herself.

"Michelle, "Larry stammered, "I've gotten into my own business, and I'd like you to come over tomorrow night so I can tell you all about the opportunity! How about it?" "What kind of business is it?" Michelle asked.

"Just come to my house and you will find out" Michelle pressed for more information but was unsuccessful.

She then remembered talking to a girl friend that had complained about some of the tactics that certain Amway distributors had used to get her to go to a meeting. Michelle sensed the possibility that this might be such a ploy and so the asked Larry, "Is it Amway?"

Larry hesitated, smiled and then exclaimed, "No, it's just a great business opportunity. How about us getting together, and I'll tell you all about it?" She agreed to attend the meeting the following night. Michelle arrived promptly at 7:30 p.m. After Larry had lectured for an hour and a half about the fantastic opportunities the business had to offer with the possibility of earning an income to match one's dreams, one fellow finally asked, "What is this business called?" Larry replied eagerly, "The American Way!" "Oh, you mean Amway!" the man concluded. Michelle was devastated. "How could Larry have lied to me!" she thought. Something strange seemed to have gotten a hold of her friend. For months everywhere he went he carefully concealed the name Amway in an attempt to recruit others into this organization.

"I felt used!" Michelle exclaimed to me. "When I tried to talk to Larry about it, he just wouldn't listen. Because I didn't join, he felt I was a loser and that my way of thinking was totally negative. The only thing he would talk about whenever I saw him was his Amway business, even at church! This business has really affected our relationship. Our friendship has never been the same."

Another girl, whose name was Jessie, related to me her experience with this business. She told me how one day some of her old Schoolmates from a Bible college in California had called her "out of the blue." These friends, now married and living in Central Oregon, were very anxious to get together with Jessie and seemed more than willing to make the long drive over the Cascade Mountains to Portland, Oregon, to see her. Jessie eagerly looked forward to an evening of reminiscing and fellowship with these friends. She was, indeed, very disappointed when she found out that the reason these guests had driven hundreds of miles was to try to sponsor her in to the Amway business.

Michelle's and Jessie's stories are not unique. For the past two years, I have carefully collected dozen of stories similar to theirs — only the names and places have changed. But let's go a step further. I have also discovered that thousands, like Larry, have eventually dropped out of this business. In fact, more than 50 percent of the total distributors quit in any given year. I'm sure that they felt like failures, and that is understandable. Most sales companies reward only those who produce results. The evidence shows that the vast majority of Amway distributors really earn very little, while a very small percentage of the entire one million distributors enjoy enormous profits. These tremendous adverse odds are not obstacles to those with this mission and its accompanying dream. Despite the world's situation, they are single minded in their determination.

Everyday newspapers, radio and TV bring us more bad news. The world is shaking at its very foundations. Famine, drought and rumors of war threaten to engulf us all. Skyrocketing inflation and unemployment push us to the brink of chaos. Yet there are those among us who are dedicated to a dream. The dream is that they are going to make it and make it big in this business. Unfortunately, in most cases, it is only a dream. It will probably never come true.

CHAPTER 2

Getting Started

It was a misty Sunday evening in the month of May when my wife Victoria and I followed Mark and Denise Hall, our upline sponsors, into their motel room in Eugene, Oregon. Mark, a full-time evangelist, had just concluded a speaking engagement for a local congregation. Accompanying our party was Millie Hooper, a well-known gospel singer, and Don and Melissa Griffin, close personal friends of ours. We all pushed into the small, but attractively decorated, room only to quickly discover a lack of seating. We opted for the adjoining bed.

As soon as Mark closed the door, he focused his gaze towards me. Then, and very much the same way that he would open a sermon, he threw his arms outright and began to exclaim. "Phil, you must become a Direct Distributor before September! Don't get me wrong. You're doing a great job, but you are going to have to sponsor a lot more people into this business if you want to make it! Lester Canon wants you to be the guest speaker at his convention this fall. There will probably be over 15,000 people present. Can you imagine that? As an author, just think of all the money you'll make selling your books! You will need a semi trailer full of books to accommodate this crowd!" (Not until much later did I realize the full impact of his emphasis on selling books.)

Our eyes remained riveted on Mark as he stormed back and forth across the room delivering his message.

"Phil, you have to be there I You won't believe this mob. They are the wildest and most excited group of people you will ever witness in your entire life. When Lester stands up and commands them to go to the back of the room and buy books, they obey! It's crazy, but it's fool proof. It's simple. You'll walk out of that convention with a suitcase full of money!"

By now Mark was in a complete frenzy of excitement, walking briskly around the room waving his arms descriptively through the air. "Man, they'll fill their arms full with books. They'll buy them by the case and run home to give them to their friends, downlines and anyone even remotely interested in this business." Mark never let up. He pressed on. Now leaning across the bed, gesturing with his right hand, he continued. "Listen to me, Phil I Last year I walked out of Lester's convention with two briefcases full of money from selling motivational books. I made over $100,000 in cash in one night. We're talking about megabucks. "You can do the same thing. I'm counting on you now. You have to break 'Direct' before September."

Mark turned towards Miss Hooper. "And Millie, if you were to get into this fabulous organization, I'm sure that with your notoriety as a singer, Lester would invite you, too. Just think of all the albums you could selling". Millie looked at Mark with a big questioning expression, probably because she had absolutely no idea what the Amway business was all about. However, her reply reflected her deep and sincere faith in God. "Albums, Mark? You really believe that the only reason I would attend a function of that size is to sell albums? Only one thing would thrill my heart—seeing souls saved for the kingdom." Mark's face registered embarrassment.

I myself felt rather ashamed participating in this conversation, especially since only an hour before we were in a service together giving praise to God. Subsequent experiences, such as the one this evening, would continually shed more light on the perceived motives of Amway's top distributors. I had not realized until that night that the money the really big money could be made in selling books, records, tapes and other items, not directly associated with Amway. Mark Hall, who is now an Emerald Direct, is sponsored directly under Lester Canon, Crown Direct who in the past has sat on the Board of the prestigious Amway Distributors' Association. This is a separate unincorporated organization, which works in conjunction with the Amway Corporation.

Mark was always telling me much about Lester Canon. He wanted to make it clear in my mind how important and influential this man is. As far as he was concerned, I was not to forget it!

Lester is considered legendary among his Amway distributors and has become to the masses a symbol of accomplishment, achievement and ultimate success. Here was a commoner who pulled himself up by his own bootstraps to become a self-made aristocrat. His vast accumulation of wealth today is not a privilege or birthright.

Canon is well known for his incredible ability to organize some of the largest and noisiest Amway meetings in the nation. These are fully supercharged, highly motivating events with attendance often running in excess of 15,000 distributors.

Mark himself has become widely known in Amway circles. He and Lester are constantly flying back and forth across the country to address their disciples at these large functions.

Prior to this meeting in the motel room, we had been in the business about five months, and already there were certain business practices and philosophical viewpoints with, which my wife and I did not agree. One of the practices which Lester always instructed, but annoyed me the most, was never to reveal the name of the company until after you had the prospect go through an "opportunity" meeting. This was called the curiosity approach. Another favorite viewpoint frequently expressed by various leaders is that the wife should never interfere with the husband's decisions in this business. It is said that this philosophy is Biblical, and supposedly, one is not expected to flinch when it was screamed at meetings, "Wives, keep your mouths shut!" Clearly, the Bible says, "Husbands love your wives as Christ loved the church, and wives submit yourselves unto your husbands as unto Christ." So far as we were concerned, there were abuses expressed here in the area of wives' submitting to their husbands. Sure, it's important for the wife to submit to her husband, but voluntarily! It should be an act of love.

But somehow, somewhere along the line, many of the leaders of this organization went beyond just selling soap. They wanted to control the lives of their downlines—even the most personal aspects. It's a well-known fact that many of Amway's leaders are very chauvinistic. This philosophy has become common among certain lines of sponsorship.

One friend who is still in the business commented on this subject of abusive submission in this fashion. "These people know exactly what they're doing. Surely, you don't think they want the wives opening up their husbands' blind eyes, do you?"

Many questions and doubts kept coming to our minds. Was this business really for us? Could we be as successful as we were led to believe—with hard work, of course? Why weren't we allowed to build our own business the way we saw best—by emphasizing the retail selling of products? It seemed that we were always subjected to the unquestioned direction of our upline sponsors. This was not only true for myself, but it was widely known through certain lines of sponsorship in the Amway Empire—that you are to be completely loyal to your upline. Somehow I never could feel comfortable reporting to a single sovereign authority like Lester Canon. From the very beginning, I struggled with these powers to be.

During our drive home after our visit with Mark and Denise that night, my wife and I began to reflection the evening's events and how we had gotten caught up into this fast moving, fast talking business. We were beginning to get a better understanding of something very important: How the really big money was made. I had sponsored so many of our closest friends and relatives during the last several months, but we were continually hearing a common complaint from most of them—the high cost of participating in this business. There was, at rallies and meetings, a constant emphasis on the purchase of non-Amway produced motivational tools such as books and tapes. In addition, the monthly expenditures for rallies were outrageous.

Up until this evening I had dismissed these grumblings simply as misunderstandings. Mark had assured me that these books, tapes and rallies were, in fact, valuable tools needed to build the business. I believed as I had been taught—that my downlines needed to trust me the way I trusted Mark and Lester. Never before had it occurred to me that those at the top may have had an ulterior motive for our purchasing these non-Amway produced items, many of which are downplayed and described simply as motivational tools.

I trusted my sponsor Mark explicitly. He had assisted me in a previous business venture, which proved to be more than successful. "Undoubtedly he could also instruct me in how to build a successful business like his," I thought. "After all, Lester had said many times, 'Success breeds success.'"

Before, it was the unquestioning faith and loyalty to a friend. But now that was all beginning to change. There were questions and doubts coming to my mind. I needed answers.

I pulled the car into our driveway and turned off the ignition. All I could hear was the patter of rain droplets hitting the metal and glass of my Ford. I reached over and pulled my wife closer to me. Quietly we sat together, reflecting on what we had seen and heard. We now realized that there was a darker side to this business. We looked back on how it all began—the first time I met Lester Canon!

The place was Chicago, Illinois, and it was a stormy and dark winter day in December. The roads were covered with black ice, and the rain would freeze as it fell. Mark picked me up at the airport, and together, in his big Cadillac sedan, we slid cautiously and quietly across the ice. Never before had I been to Mark's home. It was a massive and impressive split-level, nestled in a park like setting.

"Phil, look, I've got to get dressed. You go on into the den and find something to read. Okay? I have a friend coming over whom I would like you to meet. His name is Lester Canon!"

Well, Lester did not arrive that evening. I did not get a chance to meet him until the following morning. I had no idea who this man was nor what his affiliation was with Mark.

I remember the doorbell ringing and Mark exclaiming excitedly, "That must be Les and Sherry!" Mark grabbed my arm and together we walked to the door while he quietly murmured under his breath, "Phil, this guy is a multi-millionaire. He's stinking rich, and he's got important friends in government and big business all over the country. "Mark was really trying to impress me with this man's wealth and influence. When the door opened, there stood before us a rather cheerful looking fellow, tall and strong in stature, with a strikingly attractive blonde on his arm.

"Come on in, Sherry. Come on in, Lester." Mark closed the door behind them and made the introductions. "Sherry, Les, this is Phil Kerns. He's the fellow I have told you all about. We're going to be doing great things together, Phil and I." Mark motioned us on ahead. "Let's all go to the kitchen. The girls can drum us up some breakfast." Mark's kitchen was really cramped, but that was okay. We just crowded around the small dinette set. I surmised we were not eating in the formal dining room in order to spare the cleaning later. Together Lester and I pulled the small table away from the wall. He smiled and sat down.

Here I was sitting across the table from a man whom I had never laid eyes on before, and Mark was standing before me giving a long dissertation on the wealth, riches and influence of this person. Mark never let him get a word in edgewise. At the time I thought it was all crazy. Mark went on to tell me that Lester, whom I could have reached over and touched, was worth more than 80 million dollars! He owned not just one, but rather an entire fleet of Rolls Royces, a bank, and a home with over 10,000 square feet.

I began to wonder if Mark was embarrassing this man. I watched Mark as he walked back and forth through the kitchen explaining how Lester had made his fortune selling SOAP! Mark roared in laugher. It was an absolutely nutty scenario. Was this really happening? I peered over my shoulder behind me. Sherry and Denise were frying and eating bits and pieces out of the pan. In front of me strolled Mark, now shouting the praises of this man, intermittently stuffing raisin toast into his mouth. "Why was it so important for me to know of this man's wealth?" I thought. My thoughts immediately were expressed in a somewhat watered down question: "Mark, why are you telling me all of this?" "It's simple, Phil," Mark replied. "I believe you could be a smashing success in this business. You're an articulate speaker. You have thousands of friends who love you. You're an author of a best seller.

Look at what this soap business has done for the Canons! They're rolling in the dough!" Mark gestured towards

Lester. "Show him your bank roll, Les," Mark began laughing all over again. I was certain that mark had now devastated this man with his embarrassing request. Lester rolled his head back and forth, hesitated slightly, and then with what appeared to be some sort of reluctance, he replied, "Well, okay Mark." Mark took the liberty and reached down by Lester's belt. From a small leather case sitting on the chair next to Lester's side, he pulled out a thick stack of $100 bills. There were several packets of crisp new mint fresh bills with $5,000 bands around them. I couldn't believe it! I'm sure my astonishment was apparent. Mark goaded me on "Look Phil, over $50,000 in CASH! Do you want to touch it? Go ahead. it's real—really—real. Do you get to carry spending money like that around back home? I'll bet your property management business doesn't allow you that luxury, does it?" Mark continued with his laughter as he removed a couple of the bands. He spread the $100 bills all over the table in an apparent effort to emphasize the huge amount of money before us. He threw some of the bills in the air, and his laughter continued. Finally Lester spoke. "Phil, what Mark is trying to tell you is that we would like to make you a millionaire!" "He wanted to make me a what?" I thought. "Okay, explain it, Mark. I want to hear how you are going to make me into a millionaire!" I exclaimed. Now I was laughing, mostly in disbelief. My thoughts continued, "Is he going to write me a check? Is that how he is going to make me a millionaire?" Mark quit laughing and quieted down. Lester then took charge. "Phil, I'll do the explaining, all right?" Lester's tone had changed. I could see he was serious. He meant business. Lester gave me a brief history of the company and its yearly success— from its birth in 1959 to the present.

He told me he grew up very poor and was just looking for an opportunity like this in order to buy the things he so desperately wanted for his family. He motioned to his wife, who sat down next to him. He took her hand and gently pulled it out in front of me so I could seethe enormous diamond set in white gold. If I remember correctly, he said that it was worth over $100,000. I couldn't believe the size of it. He then reached out to her slender neck and cupped his hand under the huge diamond that hung there in a manner of proud display. He went on to tell me that he could buy anything he wanted in the world. It didn't matter what the price was. He said it was like a dream come true. His wife, interrupting, told a story to emphasize what her husband was saying. A few weeks earlier she had left a $20,000 diamond ring in a restroom while washing her hands. Only after they had left the restaurant and were driving down the road did she miss it. They turned around and drove back, but the ring was gone. "Oh, well," Sherry said, "we will just buy another one." "And listen, Phil," Lester went on, "this same kind of opportunity is yours. You could have anything you want in the world. The choice is yours." When I looked up, I realized that everyone was now seated. All were looking at me expectantly. Quiet but anxious looks were on their faces. Each face was waiting for my decision. I was stunned. This was all happening so fast. Never in my life had I been offered the opportunity to live in the seven digit realm. "Well, okay, I'll do it." I replied hesitantly. "But what do I have to do?" Mark sprang to his feet. "Whoopee, Phil, you'll never regret it. We're on our way!" "On our way? I don't even know how the business works!" I shouted back. "Don't worry about a thing, Phil," Lester reassured me. "I'm going to call one of my associates in Miami, Florida. He'll beat you home this coming Monday night. You just make sure you have a house full of people there. Okay? He will explain everything."

That same afternoon I was the guest of the Canons and the Halis for lunch. Then, that evening, I attended my first rally with Lester and Mark, who were the guest speakers.

The following morning I flew home. The moment I stepped off the plane I began rambling to my wife a hundred miles an hour about this wonderful and crazy soap business we were getting into. I presented her with the small gift I had purchased from a concession at Lester's and Mark's rally. It was nothing extravagant—a small diamond encircled with a cluster of emeralds, They explained to me that bringing in wholesale jewelers to these events was a courtesy service and a common practice. "Honey, I think we're onto something big! You know how I have always wanted to get away from this property management business and have some freedom. I think this might be it!" Here she expressed a mixture of joy and apprehension. I could not answer her questions. That didn't matter much, though. Gene Williams, an associate of Lester's, was coming to our home on Monday night to explain the whole plan. The only thing that I really understood was that we had to make up a "success" list. This was a potential recruiting list of individuals we would invite over to our home—everyone we knew who uses soap. My wife seemed more than willing to assist by making some telephone calls. Besides I had already won her over with my small token of love and my enthusiastic description of the possibility of financial independence.

CHAPTER 3

Ain't It Great?

D ream, dream, dream!" Those were the words Gene Williams used to begin our first in-home presentation or "opportunity" meeting as it is often called. He explained how through this business, we would be able to fulfill our wildest dreams.

"Just what is it you want in life? "he asked. "Is it a college education for your children? Is it a Caribbean cruise? May be it's a new home, or even a Cadillac? May be you would just like to have more money to give to missions or charitable organizations. What ever your dream is, no matter how large, it will be well within your reach with this opportunity!"

Our first Amway meeting was considered a success. At least Gene felt that it was successful. We had sponsored three couples from the group who showed up. "I'd travel across the country to sponsor just one person," Gene said in his deep Southern drawl, "because one person is like a million dollars in the bank!" Gene was not by any means a dynamic speaker. He stammered and had difficulty with his words. Yet some how through his acrobatic abuse of the English language, he was able to keep everyone rolling in their seats, halfway between pain and laughter.

When the meeting was over, Gene invited those who had questions to stay. I stood to the rear of the room and bid those leaving good night. I was flabbergasted when one of my dearest friends whispered in my ear, "Phil, this guy's a con artist."

A long-time business acquaintance boldly denounced the evening's event as a "waste of time—a ridiculous get-rich ploy." "Haven't you ever heard of the pyramid schemes?" he retorted with a smirk. "But, but it's not a pyramid," I stuttered, taken back by his reaction. Another man walked directly up to me and growled, "Why didn't you tell me it was Amway in the first place?" He then stormed out of the room.

I didn't expect these types of reactions. I was only doing as instructed by Lester and Mark. It seemed like everyone was leaving. I was baffled. Some left quietly, with no comment. Others told me they had already been in Amway and shook their heads in disappointment as they left. Those who were going had made up their minds. They wanted nothing to do with this venture. Either they had heard the plan before or had made a value judgment of the speaker's presentation. Some were just not interested.

I felt bad. Most of those I had invited were family friends and close business acquaintances. This really bothered me. I had so many questions. After all, what did I even know about the business?

On reflection, Gene really didn't say much that night, even though he did a lot of talking. He brought no products. He brought no literature. As a matter of fact, he brought nothing except this smartly dressed self, wearing boots with an 18-carat gold tips and a pin stripe suit. All he did was talk and draw circles—lots and lots of circles.

"Each circle," he had explained, "represents $100." Soon he had duplicated enough of these spheres and drew enough connecting tentacles to allow us to earn $96,000 or more. The possibilities were unlimited!

"What kind of rut are you in today?" Gene had asked the group. "I'll bet many of you here are on the S.I.A. Budget. You know, the 'Spend It All Budget!' Well, with this business you can quit your job in 90 days. You can be financially independent in two years. There are only three ways you can fail, Detailitis, Excusitis and Procrastination!..."

Comments like these had enticed the three couples who remained to hear more. They finally left around 1:30p.m., but only after Gene had made certain to schedule meetings for the min their own homes that same week. It was now time to drill Gene for answers. He could sense my anxiety. I explained to him the reactions I received from those who left the meeting earlier.

"Phil, you are worrying about absolutely nothing. Not everyone is going to get into this business! Besides, you just wait. As soon as you become successful, they'll all jump in, too. Happens all the time." That was not my concern. I felt I had to explain.

"They're my friends, Gene, and my family. They really believe they were being used or something." "In this business, Phil, you will find out who your real friends are! Some people are just born losers. Everyone is not a winner. You're a winner. just hang in there!"

His answer did not fully satisfy me. "But, then, maybe Gene was right," I thought. "Maybe they were just negative." Anyway, I had already committed myself to this venture, and I had to find out what it was all about. Even Lester must have felt that I could be successful in this business. He had sent Williams all of the way from Miami, Florida, to Oregon just to hold this meeting.

(I feel I must make this point clear. Never for a moment did I see my beloved family or friends as "losers." As a matter of fact, statements like this, together with other tactics to be explained later, eventually caused me to withdraw from the business.).

The Amway opportunity up to this point was not easy for me to understand. In my mind, there were just lots and lots of circles. So far, I had heard nothing but fantastic speeches by Lester, Mark and Gene on how I could become rich. All of the emphasis was on how much money could be made and on how successful one could be. No one ever told me anything about the products or how to sell them. But how was it going to happen? I needed more information and facts. My upline sponsor was almost three thousand miles to the east, and this presented a communication problem. Fortunately, when I called Mark I found him home. "Mark, I sure appreciate all of the assistance you and Lester have given me so far in this business. . ." Mark interrupted, "Phil, you're doing great! Gene Williams and I just talked, and he said you had 35 people present. That's fantastic! I've never had a downline with a start like that. Boy, wait until Lester hears this. He'll be very impressed!"

"Mark," I interrupted. "I still don't understand what is going on. Gene Williams never really explained how this business works. He just drew circles on a board and told us we all could become a Direct Distributor in 90 days. I need a manual. I need some sort of literature. I'd like to see what the products look like. I'd like to know how good the products are. I haven't even seen a box of soap. After all, isn't Amway known as a soap business?" I could hear Mark chuckling on the other end of the line.

Then he quit laughing, and in a serious tone he said, "Now listen to me. You don't need that manual at all. Lester says it was simply written to satisfy the Federal Trade Commission. And, besides, if you sit around reading that manual, you'll get all confused. You won't be out sponsoring people." "Mmm," I replied. I listened quietly as Mark encouraged me. His voice made me feel more reassured. He always had an uncanny way of making one see things his way. I explained to Mark the disappointing reactions I had received from my family and friends. Mark continued, "Look, Phil, you're getting help from the top people in the business. Lester wants to see you make 'Direct' really bad. He even paid Williams a $5,000 honorarium to make your speaking engagement! Who are you going to listen to anyway? How can you expect to get good advice from your family and friends? Are they successful? Aren't you going to listen to the advice of someone who is successful?" - Mark took another breath and finished. "You don't need to read a manual. I'm sending more speakers to Portland to help you. They'll explain everything. We'll build this business together. Williams will be back, and I will have an Emerald from Olympia come down to personally help you. Don't give up! Okay? Just sponsor, sponsor, sponsor. Build that organization! Listen, there are very few people in the business who receive first-class treatment like this. You should take advantage of it. If you are having any doubts about the business, look, even Pat Boone is in it. I'll call you next week. Bye!" I felt better after having listened to Mark.

In the following weeks, everything happened just as Mark said it would. Our business was frequently visited by guest speakers like Tim Sevrson of Olympia, now a Diamond Direct; Mark Hall, Emerald Direct, our sponsor; and, of course, Gene Williams, Diamond Direct and Lester's associate of Miami, Florida.

For additional assistance, my wife and I were plugged into a Northwest organization headed by Tom Kenney, Diamond Direct. Mark had felt it to be to our advantage to have help close by, and he was searching for the ideal couple. He explained that Lester had real clout, and anything he told his distributors to do, no matter what, they would do. Therefore, providing assistance for us was no problem for Lester. If he requested it, it was done.

Each evening, Monday through Friday, we held meetings. This went on week after week, religiously, as instructed by my team of experts. At the conclusion of each meeting, I made arrangements with those interested in the business to have a meeting in their home the following night, if possible, or sometime during that week. The amazing thing about all of this is that up to this point I had never seen a product, signed a document nor read a manual of instruction. As a matter of fact, it was almost eight weeks before we received our first kits, which included a variety of Amway products and some motivational materials. When the kits finally did arrive, I did just as Mark said. I threw the manual in the trashcan, and every time I sponsored others, I instructed them to do the same.

One day Mark called to tell me that he had found the ideal couple to assist us. They were Mr. and Mrs. Terry Bayer of Portland, Oregon. The Bayers were in the Kenney's "line of sponsorship" and were more than happy to help us in building our Amway distributorship. I remembered the first night I was invited to the Bayers' home. Their "office" was wall-to-wall cassettes. Terry had a complete library of tapes on speakers in various lines of sponsorship. There must have been, in my estimation, over 150 titles. The garage had shelf after shelf of various Amway products. It was an impressive display of inventory, obviously worth thousands of dollars. The Bayers urged us to go to the rallies, seminars and all other upcoming events sponsored by their line. Together my wife and I attended these meetings, and we invited those we had recruited to go, too. It was life in the fast lane. Sponsor, schedule that person for a meeting the next night, if possible, and again at this next meeting look for a gleam in someone's eyes. Sponsor that one, move to their house the next night, give another meeting and so on.

It was just as Williams said. Before long some of those who were negative in the beginning began to jump aboard simply because they saw I could sponsor people. One such person was my father-in-law. This caused utter disbelief throughout my immediate family. I kept at it, however, and eventually I also recruited my own father. One by one other members of my family wanted to get in.

It seemed as if everyone became my target. No one could carry on a conversation with me unless they were somehow invited to an "opportunity" meeting. I spoke with doctors, lawyers, dentists and building developers. I didn't stop there. Every restaurant waitress was subjected to my dissertation. Every airline stewardess was delayed until she had heard about this business.

On one occasion I flew into Atlanta, Georgia, Lester's hometown, to go on a television program to talk about my book, People's Temple, People's Tomb, and my experiences with Jim Jones, the cult leader. Mark had told me that I would find one of Lester's limousines out front to pick me up. When I walked outside the terminal, I saw that there were three black Cadillac limousines. Each one was spotlessly clean and highly polished. The license plates said, "LES 1, LES 2 and LES 3." I was really confused so I went over to LES 1 and asked the chauffeur, "Which car am I supposed to ride in?" He smiled and said, "This one will do." As we drove through Atlanta, I must admit that I wondered if Lester had sponsored this guy. "Better not ask," I thought to myself. "He would probably tell Lester I tried to recruit him." By now I was really good at presenting this opportunity to others. I found I could schedule seven out of every ten people with whom I spoke to come to a meeting. I drew those silly circles on everything-napkins, table tops and even candy bar wrappers. Sometimes if I were in a jam and couldn't find a scrap of paper in order to tutor my new prospect, I would just use the back of my hand.

I found myself, in a matter of less than 90 days, giving meetings through this domino process all throughout the states of Oregon, Washington and eventually Florida. I flew to Miami, Tampa and Key West in one week.

My normal office hours in our property management business were from 8 a.m. to 5 p.m. five days a week. My second shift, the Amway business, began at 7 p.m. and commonly ended around midnight seven days a week. Being away from our business as much as I was had taken its toll. But that was a storm I was willing to weather for success. Every spare minute was spent in talking, listening and dreaming about Amway. We had purchased a number of cassette tapes at different rallies and conventions, and we would listen to them in the car while driving to and from these events. Don't think I wasn't excited. I most certainly was. I was building an organization. Lester and Mark kept telling me to "Believe in the Dream!" I guess you might say I was becoming a believer.

"Look at all the people we've sponsored into this business and those who are interested in possibly joining, Vicky!" I exclaimed to my wife. She did not share my enthusiasm. Instead she peered out the plane's window at the ocean below. We were preparing to land in San Juan, Puerto Rico. This was once home to my wife. She had grown up here as a child, nourished on the tropical sugar cane and mangoes.

She turned to me and rested her head on my shoulder. I could see the tears welling up in her eyes. Concerned, I asked, "What is it, Honey?"

"Do you really think that Jesus wants us in this business?"

"I'm really not sure, Sweetheart." Her question had good reason to make me feel guilty because I really hadn't given it much thought. "All I know is that it is a great opportunity. The door appears to be open, and the possibilities are unlimited. Besides, if we do earn a million dollars as Les and Mark say, then we'll have so much more we can share with those in need."

My wife's tears now flowed down her cheeks. I put my arm around her and held her close to me. She laid her head on my shoulder. At that moment, I began to seriously question what this business was all about.

"You don't really believe all that talk about losers do you, Phil, just because they decide not to join? Many of these people are our dearest friends." My wife reminded me how disgusted I had often felt when listening to so many of the speakers at various functions. I remember the night we attended a rally where John Wells, Triple Diamond, was the guest speaker, John is in Lester Canon's line of sponsorship. it was a Sunday and thousands were now attending John's meeting, which was advertised as a non-denominational Christian service. I remember John, seemingly self-composed, as he walked up to center stage in his all white tuxedo. He stood there for the longest time; his arms hung next to his side as he stared out at the audience.

Then, suddenly, in what appeared to be an agitated display of emotional anger, he wrestled his white jacket from his back. As the audience recoiled into their seats in unbelief, he simultaneously threw his coat clear across the stage in great animation. With his left arm stretched out, he shook his tighten fist towards the ceiling and screamed, "Get out of here, Satannnnn!" I looked around the large auditorium. With this fit of nervous discomposure, he had succeeded in capturing the attention of every person in the room. Face after face focused on John in complete silence. He continued by expounding on the virtues of this business and how God had blessed it in such a wonderful way. I guess you might say his speech was a total reflection of his philosophy—PROSPERITY. To John, poverty appeared to be a demonic trait. He went on for over an hour that particular night, hammering away at all dissenters and critics of the business. As far as John Wells was concerned, there was only one rational decision to make and that was to either be in Amway or be stupid! John's statements on other occasions could be construed to some as contradictive of his public testimony of being a Christian.

"If you're broke, you've got to be stupid!" he screamed to the crowd. "But you see, most people are too stupid to realize the disease they have called Stinkin' Thinkin'! Stupid Stinkin' Thinkin'!"

After reflecting on this particular meeting and others where similar thoughts and statements were expressed, my wife and I began to discuss the tapes we so often were asked to listen to (and pay for). One particular excerpt came to mind where John Wells was speaking at a Tampa, Florida, rally. "Some of you may think I'm a kook, but I'm a rich kook!" He went on to proclaim proudly that he had earned $70 million plus that year, and then, very boldly, he challenged the crowd, "Anyone out there want to criticize that? Put that in your pipe and smoke it!"

These kinds of comments were irritating to us; they had crept in and touched a very sensitive part of our lives. They seemed like arrogant statements laced with bigotry. My wife reminded me what the Bible says, "You will know God's people by their love." (I John 4:7-8)

The scriptures also read, "if a man says he loves God and hates his brother whom he has seen, how can he love God whom he has not seen?" (I John 4:20) These were Biblical truths we could not ignore.

As the plane sped silently through the sky, I remembered the story in the Bible of the woman who gave her last two pennies. The Bible says God considered her gift to be more precious than all the money that the rich boaster had given. I believe God was speaking to me to get my priorities in order and give what I possessed now no matter how small the amount. To Him, little things are worth just as much, especially if the gift comes from the heart.

I was more determined than ever to find out what the business was all about. I needed to think on my own — not just listen to Mark and Lester. I didn't want to admit that the Amway toothpaste tasted like glue and cost twice as much as the drugstore brand. I didn't want to confess that my retention rate of those whom I had sponsored in the business was really poor or that I was constantly having to pump them up to keep them in. Did I really need a million dollars? Didn't God say He would supply all our needs? Did I need success to fulfill my life? Besides, where was all my success? I sure couldn't see it. As a matter of fact, I was spending a fortune for gas, telephone bills and airfare in order to sponsor all those people on my "success" list. What did the bottom line say that month? $7.78 net. Hard to believe? Well, it's true!

CHAPTER 4

Behind the Curtain

It was a Friday afternoon when Mark and I arrived at the Portland Coliseum. The parking lots were vacant, but I knew that by 7 p.m. it would be havoc trying to find a space. This was "West Coast Free Enterprise Day," the biggest and most exciting event of the year for Amway distributors in the Northwest. It was going to be held in the home arena of the NBA Portland Trailblazers.

Mark had called from Chicago, Illinois, and asked that I attend. He said he wanted some assistance in coordinating the book sales. I felt this would be my golden opportunity to see firsthand how such an event was put together. Soon I was to learn that it was a methodically well rehearsed program. I sat and listened as Tom Kenney, Diamond Direct, who is in John Wells' line of sponsorship, gave orders to workers inside the arena. He had them position the speakers' platform and arrange the folding chairs into neat rows in front of the stage. Then Tom called everyone together to discuss each person's respective part in the program. How long should the band play? Who would be the first speaker? Do we have all the doors covered with individuals to handle tickets and security? Tom covered every detail. Nothing was left to chance. Before the night was over, he would relinquish his position as foreman, shed his shirtsleeves and slacks and return in his best evening attire as the host of this magnificent program. All this activity was designed to give the Northwest distributors the most exciting extravaganza that they had ever experienced. After purchasing tickets, a program and possibly a tape packet to take home, it would be easy for a distributor to drop over $50 for the evening. The people who were attending tonight were coming to witness something spectacular. They wanted to see success, hear success, feel success and touch success. They were not to be disappointed. People started filtering in the large auditorium about 6 p.m. By 7:30 there were in excess of 10,000 people there. Before 8 p.m. the coliseum appeared to be packed. People were crowded in like sardines. At 8p.m.sharp the band struck up with the "Rocky Theme." The lights were dimmed, and the mood was set. Tom Kenney stood next to the exit door, rubbing his hands together with great anticipation as he waited for his introduction. "And now, Ladies and Gentlemen...," the announcer bellowed, "that moment you have all been waiting for. I'd like to present to you our host, Diamond Direct, Tommmmm Kenney!"

The trumpets blared even louder than beforehand the drums once again beat out that famous "Rocky Theme." It was a song of victory. Tom Kenney sprang from the exit and broke out into a full run as he raced down the isle and up to center stage. The crowd rose to their feet. People cheered and whistled. I had never seen anything like it in my life. The roof literally came off the place. It was louder than any Blazer basketball game. No presidential candidate would receive this kind of applause. It went on for a full two minutes. It seemed like ten.

Then, when Tom Kenney introduced John Wells, Triple Diamond, the crowd once again sprang to their feet, screaming and clapping with great enthusiasm. It was a thunderous response. It kept getting louder and louder. The crowd began to push forward towards the stage like a mob trying to get into a Tokyo subway train. Cameras were flashing, hands were being thrusted out and books and programs were being waved, requesting an autograph. "So this is what it is all about!" I remembered thinking to myself. Even though I had been to a number of rallies, I, too, had been caught up in the emotion of the moment. This time, however, I needed to be more objective. I didn't waste any time. I wanted to analyze what was making this all happen. It wasn't going to be easy, but I had to get backstage. Pearl and Ruby Directs, loyal to Tom Kenney, were posted carefully in this area, seemingly acting as guards. As I walked down the long corridor, the screams and applause continued. "If only there was a way I could get past that guard," I thought. "Of course — Mark. He is one of the guest speakers. He can get me backstage." it didn't take me long before I had tracked him down. He was busy in the hall supervising the sale of motivational books. I explained to Mark that I wanted a ringside seat backstage. I wanted to see these stars up close. Mark obliged and together we hurried downstairs. It was a simple matter for Mark, since he was a star speaker, to introduce me to everyone and thus allow me the privilege of complete freedom all around the platform as well as backstage. Now leaning on the stage, I had a bird's eye view of everything. I could hear the various Diamonds in another room arguing about who was going to get what share of the booty from this event. I watched Tom's wife, Debbie Anne Kenney, scurry back and forth with proceeds from the ticket sales. She was stacking money upon a table and seeking the assistance of others to count it. Most of the tickets, I was told, were sold prior to this particular event. However, tickets could still be purchased at the gates. Walking around backstage like this required that I always act positive, especially since I was not wearing a Diamond pin. These people possessed a keen ability to discern if one was with them or against them. I knew full well how Tom Kenney perceived those who were negative or those who questioned, even in the slightest way, his leadership. "Just flush them!" he would say, matter of factly. As far as he was concerned, there would be no heretics in his group. Now one can understand why I spent the entire evening with a bigger-than-life smile pasted across my face. I knew that if I wanted to gain some insight into this business, I had to conceal my indifference and possible suspicions.

It was, indeed, a very interesting evening. Up on stage there was much talk of villas, cruises, expensive cars, banking practices and upcoming events. In the hallways, tables were heaped full of tapes, books and lots of American memorabilia. Events similar to this could go on all day and all weekend. Were there spin-offs? You bet. The record breaking ticket sales, catered dinners, books and cassettes were just a few. Others include soft drinks, hot dogs, calendars and even bumper stickers. At some of these events, it was not uncommon to see additional spin-offs such as the sale of suits, jewels and automobiles. All of these were considered "tools of the trade"-even custom tailored suits. Whoever sponsored the event was like any well-schooled promoter. He would make certain that he profited from absolutely everything, if possible, sold at his event. I had the opportunity to speak at some length with Dave Beach, Diamond Direct. He was an extremely sharp young man who prior to joining Amway, had been an electrical engineer. He had rapidly climbed the "ladder of success" and would, later in the evening, share with the audience some of the experiences he encountered along the way. Many questions darted to my mind as I stood back and observed. Why would Wells and Kenney bring in a Diamond all the way from New York? After all, wasn't this "West Coast Free Enterprise Day"? Why was Mark being flown from one "Free Enterprise Day" to another? My only conclusion to these questions was that it must be HYPE! The guest speakers for this event were carefully handpicked. The enthusiasm they could generate was hard to believe without witnessing it firsthand. It was a common practice to bring in outside guest speakers, not just on a "Free Enterprise Day" but all throughout the year for various rallies and seminars. This always brought a lot of fresh new "success" stories, which fueled new excitement.

These special speakers and other members of the Board of the Amway Distributors' Association constitute a small elite private club. You scratch my back, and I'll scratch yours. Some have said that the company frowns on this activity, but its use is widespread. Possibly millions of dollars each year are spent in honorariums to cover the costs of these expensive guests. The reader is probably asking himself how I can be so sure about all of this? Well, I too was asked to go out of state with all expenses paid to dazzle others in different lines of sponsorship because I was an author. It seemed that the leaders enjoyed using people of notoriety to draw crowds and breed enthusiasm in this business. This "Free Enterprise Day" event was no different. It was just on a much grander scale. Dave Beach was young, very handsome and successful. He would be well worth whatever price they paid.

Later I was to learn that the cost of these honorariums was a small price to pay in comparison to the enormous profits reaped by the host at these functions. My thoughts came back to my own business. As the meeting continued in the auditorium, I went upstairs to question Mark as he supervised the sale of hundreds of books and tape packets. "Mark, when I continually sponsor and don't retail as you have instructed, I don't make any profit. But tonight the light has really dawned on me. I have invited all my downlines to this event, and they will probably pay the asking price of $39 for your tape packet and purchase a myriad of motivational books, not to mention the admission fee, all of which will benefit no one except those putting on this gig, right?"

I did not receive a response. Mark has a unique way of ignoring a person when he wants to but can keep right on smiling as he does. Mark was now autographing motivational packets. After a few moments he finally backed away from the table. He reached out and draped his arm across my shoulders. With a squeezy clasp and a smile, Mark led me across the hall to the stadium entryway. Thousands were crammed into the stadium singing, "God Bless America."

Together we stood and watched this spectacle. Hundreds now stood many holding hands, and some gently swaying to the song's cadence. "Look, Phil, they're happy. Just look! That's what counts. You want to take that away from them?" I couldn't believe my ears. I turned and solemnly walked away from my sponsor. My wife was waiting down the hall, and together we left this event in Portland, very disillusioned. Already we had spent hundreds of dollars on rallies and seminars prior to this particular "Free Enterprise Day" Well, it wasn't free. We weren't equals. Those who organized this event would walk away with their attaché cases full of cash, just as they had previously predicted. The sponsors of these events almost always insist that tickets be paid in cash only. At many events I have seen doormen ask that checks be made out to "cash." No receipts are given.

I was now convinced how my uplines perceived this business. It was a colossal plan aimed to appeal only to selfishness and carnality: the obsession of money and things, regardless of the price. Their brief cases full of money were sufficient evidence of that. Our zeal was gone. We were now uncertain about our future in this business! I assured my wife that our friends and family members were much more important than all the money in the world.

Besides, the Amway business, as we were instructed to conduct it, was showing us little or no profit. This evening was additional proof that the big money, indeed, was being made by a very select few, and not by selling soap. Later we learned that many times these events were scheduled to be held concurrently with a function being offered by the Amway Corporation—the same date and the same city. The hosts would urge their downlines to attend their rally rather than the Amway sponsored event. Were the leaders really wanting to motivate these people, or were they wanting these individuals to spend money for their own profit? I felt I had already seen enough. Certainly over the months I had witnessed, unknowingly, millions of dollars being cleverly siphoned away from thousands of unsuspecting Amway distributors.

CHAPTER 5

Enough Is Enough!

Several days later, still reflecting on the events at the coliseum, I thought back on that night Vicky and I spent with Mark and Denise in the motel room in Eugene, Oregon. Mark's message to me was, "Become a Direct Distributor. You'll sell $100,000 worth of books in one night. You'll walk out of a rally with a briefcase full of cash."

I certainly wasn't making much money in Amway. I found it easy to sponsor people, but I couldn't get them to order or purchase products.

I went to the telephone and called Mark. "I'm tired of this, Mark. This business is a bunch of baloney. The only real money I have seen during the past 13 months is the money spent on books and tapes of which I have received absolutely no percentage—not to mention that every rally or seminar we have attended has cost us money, too."

"It's okay, Phil," Mark assured me. "Take it easy. That's all part of the program. But remember you're not selling the product. You're selling the 'Dream!' Product sales will just happen. You'll see. That will be explained to you later."

This time Mark's answer was not satisfactory. I needed to know more. Now! Not later. Besides, at the rate I was going, these "dreams" would never be fulfilled. Up to this point, they were costing me a bundle.

"Mark," I protested, "if I continue to sponsor in the fashion you and Lester suggest, I will be broke before the year is out. I need to retail in order to cover my expenses."

"No, don't retail, Phil. That's terrible," Mark interjected. "Trust me, will you? Just keep buying the products that you use and instruct your downlines to do the same."

It was time to hang up anyway. These "long distance tax deductions," as they are called in the business, were breaking me.

I was now discovering something I should have known in the first place. I really couldn't make decent profits in this business continually sponsoring and wholesaling the way Lester and Mark had instructed. It just did not pencil out. But how could I have figured it out? From the very beginning they had me so hyped up and moving so fast that I never had a chance to think. From the moment I said, "Yes, I'll join," I was being urged to sponsor as many friends and family members as I possibly could. Training? Forget it! This was a key tactic I was told. "Don't give them time to think. Just have them trust their upline and do as they are instructed."

A frequently used slogan is, "The more you know, the less you'll grow." We were also advised that whatever one does when contacting another, "Be sure you don't tell them it's Amway! You wouldn't want them to be deprived of an opportunity would you?"

I couldn't help but remember what my precious wife had said to me as we were flying into San Juan. "Do you really think Jesus wants us in this business?

What she should have been saying was, "Boy, you sure blew it this time, Phil." I was beginning to realize I had blown it, and I thank God for such an understanding wife.

Both of us agreed that we had had our fill of these Babylonian high priests preaching the gospel of gold. We were tired of seeing these self-appointed prophets strut back and forth across the stages of America daring the living God and using Him for financial gain.

I remember how at one particular event a leading distributor explained to the audience how Amway got its start in the Bible. He said it began in the "Book of Exodus." Casually he began to tell his tale with his hands tucked into his trouser pockets.

"I'm going to tell you tonight a story I haven't told you before. This is a true story, and you can al I check me out when you get back to the Hyatt because you can find this in any Gideon Bible...

"The Time God Drew Circles for Moses" The crowd burst into laugher.

"Now Moses was shepherd, herdsman and cattleman, and he was a farmer. He was the whole works. He was a forest ranger. If it got done, he had to take care of it cause it was his land; and if he didn't care about it, nobody else would.

"So Moses was on his mountain one afternoon, and he saw a bush burning, and he paused. If that fire jumped from the bush and spread to some of the other little scrub bushes on the mountain, he had a problem on his hands. He'd have to run for help, and they'd be digging ditches and fighting that blaze all across the mountaintop.

"So Moses had to watch to see if the fire would either spread or wait until it consumed the bush and went out. So he stood there for a few minutes with his hands on his hips ... but the fire didn't spread. The bush wasn't consumed. It just stuck there like glue. Moses continued to watch. He was fascinated a little at first, then disgusted. The fire stayed right there. Wouldn't go out. Wouldn't consume the bush. Moses was afraid to go on till it had done its dirty work and he could be sure; but it didn't spread either. He stood for the longest time. Finally Moses kind of tilted his head and said, 'GOD, is this AMWAAAY?'"

By now the crowd was roaring. The speaker continued, "And God said, 'Moses, if I could tell you what this is in one or two sentences, I would have told you in one or two sentences! Now I don't have time to talk about it at this moment, but it's going to take at least a couple of hours so get your shoes off. Come up here and relax. Sit down and I'll tell you what this burning bush is all about.' "Now this is true. God used the curiosity approach! I know there are some people who are against the curiosity approach, but even God used the curiosity approach. Now attracted to the burning bush, God launched into a dream session that would make Donald Chaney envious. God began to describe to Moses a land flowing with milk and honey and a place of freedom and a place where people could wake up in the morning without a chain around their necks in a land of plenty. 'And the great thing about it,' God said, as He was not describing some climbing-the-mountain success game where you get to the top and you're lonely and cynical and you've stepped all over peoples' backs to get there, but God said to Moses, 'YOU CAN TAKE YOUR PEOPLE WITH YOU! You can take your friends and your relatives and anybody who's tired of be in a slave, and they can go with you into this freedom!'

"And Moses shrugged and God began to describe the Promised Land, 'And here's how you'll get there, 'and a white board mysteriously appeared behind God. He took a magic marker, and He drew a great big circle on the board and said, 'Moses, this is youuuuu,' and drew a line with a circle at the top and said, 'I AM YOUR SPONSOR!'"

This is only one example of many similar situations. At practically every event we attended, there was someone who would figure out a way to bend, twist and malign the scriptures for financial gain. Usually it was in a "Steve Martin fashion," designed to keep the listeners in stitches. I had always tried to reassure my downlines not to be disturbed by this. We were building our own organization. Almost everyone I sponsored had a sincere and deep love for God and found the use of the scriptures in this fashion blasphemous.

I was hoping we could build our business outside of this arena, but this constant abuse of the scriptures could not be escaped. The business was absolutely full of it. Almost every tape that one would listen to seemed to have. Another religious or philosophical viewpoint. Every book seemed to shout, "You can do it. What do you need God for?"

Oh, don't get me wrong. God was in the picture. But He became "The Almighty Shelf God." Move Him from one shelf to another, using whatever shelf was most convenient. What did all of this twisted religion have to do with selling anyway?

When Vicky and I greeted Lester and Sherry at the Seattle, Washington, convention, we had more or less made up our minds to get out even if Lester was pushing hard for us to become Directs. The place was packed with thousands of screaming admirers. The band was still playing "Rocky," and I remember Lester's words after he got the crowd to calm down. He is considered by his followers to be the pinnacle of success. Each distributor in Lester's downline is taught that a key to success is to cling to his every word. Lester exhorted the audience.

"I know a lot of you here today are excited about this business. And many of you want to tell people about Jesus, but it's better to get someone in the business first and get some money in his back pocket. Then you can tell him about Jesus."

Statements like these led me to question whether or not God had now become something insignificant. He seemingly had been coolly deported and ostracized for a box of soap! I thought, "Why even bring up God unless He takes top billing?"

It was time for us to leave. We had made up our minds. No obsession for money or power would come between us and our faith in God. Lester had always insisted, "The lack of money is the root of all evil." But we knew this could not be true for the Bible itself says, "The love of money is the root of all kinds of evil." [1 Timothy 6:10, NIV]

In traveling around the United States on my schedule of speaking engagements for the People's Temple book, I had the privilege of meeting many wonderful people. Although many of them had been blessed financially, God, not money, came first in their lives. We knew God had to be first in our lives, too. As we walked out into the night's rain from that rally in Seattle, we could hear the crowd inside chanting and clapping together in unison, "We are family! Brothers, sisters, Amway, and me. We are family! Stand up everybody and sing!"

Deep inside I felt that we had to getaway from there. We did not want to bow down before this modern day Baal. This business could not become a god to us. These people were not our family. The overt demonstrations of loyal adoration we had just witnessed, as far as we were concerned, were not directed to God.

CHAPTER 6

Free At Last

Lester Canon had said on many occasions that there would come a time in this business when I could experience freedom. He was absolutely right, but not in the way he thought! After quitting, I experienced total freedom. Gene Williams was also correct when he pointed out, "In this business you will find out who your real friends are." Well, I found out who my real friends were because when I quit, they quit!

In the weeks that followed I must have confessed my blunder a hundred times over. Some of those who had avoided me like the plague because of my winsome attempts at indoctrination now curiously listened as I acknowledged, in detail, my genuine reformation. One such person was Rupert Koblegarde. Rupert is one of Portland, Oregon's first-string corporate attorneys. If he weren't such a splendid and enjoyable sort of guy, he would have most likely thrown me out the day I barged into his office declaring, "I'm free, Rupert!" "What are you free from, Phil?" Rupert mused, now leaning back in his big leather chair' "You know that soap business I was in? I quit. I feel great! For a while I was beginning to feel like a zombie all over again. I thought I could never be deceived after my experiences in the Temple.

I thought my ability to discern deception was now sharp. Now I know that I was wrong to have gotten in, but it all seemed so straight." His secretary, who momentarily had to retreat when I so suddenly burst in, stood at the door expecting an explanation. "It's okay, Dolores. Phil just had some good news to share." With that she closed the door and left us to our conversation. Rupert got up, walked over to the window and stared out to the city below. I knew how he felt about this particular business, but I was hoping he would share some of his feelings concerning my newest declaration. He just stood there holding his chin for several moments. Finally he slowly turned, looked right into my eyes and asked, "What are your plans now, Phil?" "I'm going to tell the story," I replied quickly. "What else? Someone has to tell it!" Looking over my head at the shelves of books on the wall behind me, Rupert said, "Then I have a book you need to read."

I left his office with a copy of Con Man or Saint? by John Frasca. As I walked along the Portland sidewalks, dodging the oncoming pedestrians, I thumbed briefly through the text. I couldn't believe what I was reading! Glen Turner, a hare lipped sharecropper, had borrowed $5,000 and turned it into $100 million in 24 months. He had started a cosmetics business called "Koskot." One of the characters in the book was Willie Towner of Marion, South Carolina, a dump truck driver turned super salesman. Here's an excerpt of the story:

Willie Towner strode into the room. Glen was dumbfounded. Willie never had worn a necktie in his life. Now he was wearing a suit that shimmered. He wore a pink shirt and a fancy silk tie, a darker pink than the shirt. His shoes were made of alligator skin. Is that Willie Towner who used to drive a dump truck for the county? Holy cow. Willie smiled at the small group. "Gentlemen, I'm going to show you how you can become wealthy beyond your wildest dreams. I'm going to show you how you can earn more money in a month than most people make in a year." He spoke quickly, confidently. He walked over to a small blackboard set in a corner. He pulled it to the center of the room. While he talked, he scratched astronomical numbers on the board...

There was no way I could put this book down. As soon as I got home, I continued reading and didn't stop until I had finished it about 4 a.m. The Glen Turner story was full of strikingly comparable methods and often-repeated statements which ironically are used by many Amway distributors today. Some of the most commonly used clichés are "Dream," "Believe," "Think success," "Believe in yourself," "The only way you can help yourself is by helping someone" and "Fake it till you make it!"

After reading Con Man or Saint?, I have often wondered if Amway distributors borrowed this terminology from Turner's group, or was it Turner who confiscated these words and phrases from some Amway distributors? Could it simply be a coincidence? For 24 months I dedicated countless hours in researching and compiling reams of information on the Amway Corporation, Inc. and the Amway Distributors' Association of the United States, an unincorporated association. I would eat, sleep and dream Amway—not in building a business, as before, but in finding out how it was built and how it operates!

I spoke with distributors at all levels of achievement. I interviewed scores of individuals who left the business for one reason or another—some at the Diamond level, others who were just beginners. I have read page after page of public and government testimony concerning this business. I have interviewed hundreds of distributors, many of whom have confirmed the existence of problems which I had suspected for so long. Leaving the business and now attempting to come back to collect important information was like pulling teeth. You see, quitting this business, especially in my line of sponsorship, is similar to being excommunicated from a church. Everyone associated with the organization avoids you like an epidemic. You are labeled as "one who is negative—a loser!"

If you are in John Wells' line of sponsorship, you have most likely heard John's lesson on how to handle these failures. Somehow one gets the feeling he was talking about some maggot species when he stood before the crowd and said, "I wish these dead losers would just get out. All they seem to do is lie around and stink up the place." The man who made this statement and his sponsor, Mr. Lester Canon, have both been in powerful positions as board members of the Amway Distributors' Association of which Jay VanAndel, chairman of the board, and Rich DeVos, the company's president, are also members. I believe it is important for each reader to understand the power these individuals have over their followers. The statements, which I have pointed out, are really just the tip of the iceberg! There is no doubt in my mind that these men possess some sort of charismatic power, which enables them to control such a large organization. These types of comments have had devastating and crushing effects on many of the individuals towards whom they were directed. In my estimation less than one-half of one percent of the entire assembly of distributors has and holds this unimaginable power to control others; therefore, we are talking about a very small number of people controlling a vast number of individuals.

I remember the telephone call I received from a very frantic woman in Salem, Oregon. She was calling me about my book on the Jonestown tragedy. I was new in the business, having been in only a week. "I hope that I am not disturbing you, Mr. Kerns. I go t your telephone number from your publisher in Plainsfield, New Jersey. I read your book on the People's Temple, and I just wanted to give you my condolences on the loss of your mother and sister in Jonestown. Towards the end of our telephone conversation, she asked, "Oh, by the way, are you aware of the Amway business?" "Yes," I replied, but I did not tell her I was in the business. "You know, every time I go to one of their meetings, it reminds me so much of your book—all of the chanting and the way they malign and twist the holy scriptures for gain. I feel that this business is a cult. I think you need to tell the world about this company." inside I was chuckling to myself. "This is so far from the truth thought. "This is just a soap business—an opportunity." I dismissed her statements from my mind because I felt they were unfounded and drifting somewhere between "Star Wars" and the "Twilight Zone."

However, today I know better; I wish I had not shunned this woman's notion so abruptly. I hope that if she reads this book, she will call back so I may apologize.

Could this organization be classified as a cult? There are, without a doubt, many different characteristics utilized within this integration of salespersons which could lead many individuals to arrive at the same conclusions this lady did.

I now realized there was more to this business than just soap and spin-offs. There was POWER! Amway speakers are most dynamic.

CHAPTER 7

The Investigation

There has always been an aura of mystery and intrigue to the conclaves of senior Amway distributors. One must wonder if the secrecy with which the fraternity surrounds itself is designed to keep the layman from discovering how much he knows or how much he doesn't know. One such person who desired to uncover these truths was Don Griffin, a native born Oregonian who is half Klamath Indian. He, too, was an ex-Amway distributor with an inquiring attitude for more information regarding this "inner circle."

I knew where I could find Don on a Saturday afternoon. He was coaching basketball for his church team in Portland, Oregon. When I arrived at the church gymnasium, Don looked up, waved and went on up the court to complete a fast sprint, gently demonstrating to his team a neatly tucked dunk shot. He ran over to greet me as he always did with his big bear hug. He was drenched in sweat. "What are you trying to do? Give me a shower? Where's a towel?" I teased. Don smiled. For years he had been more than a friend. He was like a brother.

"Good to see you, Phil We're still going to that Amway meeting tonight, right?"

"You bet." I replied.

"Great! I've been looking forward to this meeting all day."

"Did you get the information I needed?"

"I sure did and more, too!" The way Don answered told me he must be onto something big.

He was bouncing up and down as quickly as the basketball he had just been dribbling. "Well ,fill me in!" "You know all that bragging we've been hearing at various rallies around the country about how the Amway Corporation won great victories in court with the Federal Trade Commission?" Don asked. "Yes, yes, go on. "Well, it isn't at all what those distributors are blowing it up to be. I guess you might say it's in the eyes of the beholder. In fact, the FTC in its final order shot the company down on two key points. They said that Amway had to 'cease and desist' from two major violations. One was price fixing, and the other was misrepresentation of distributors' income." I was stunned. So far, prior to hearing this from Don, many distributors whom I knew had been led to believe that the company was the underdog and was being harassed by big government." "How can you be so sure, Don?" I asked. "It's all in black and white. I've seen the report myself. It's at the State Consumer Protection Agency. It's hot! In fact, it's really a mind blower. The report tells you everything you need to know about the entire case. It shows the complaint, the opinion of the commission who reviewed the case and, of course, the final order which tells Amway to 'cease and desist' from certain practices. I'll get you a copy this week, okay?"

(After personally reviewing the FTC report and speaking with the FTC attorneys concerning the commission's final order, it is my own opinion that this order was not a victory for the company. However, because some of the original charges were reversed, it was understandable how Amway could interpret this otherwise. One could also see how they would want to.).

"I'd sure like to know how they are complying to this final order." "Oh, they're complying all right. They have to. I have also seen a copy of Amway's compliance report—what a stack of papers! The real question should be, 'Are the one million distributors complying?' But let's not belabor that now," Don calmly replied. "Besides, we have a lot to do tonight, right? I'll see you later this evening. I've got to shower."

Don ran off across the shiny hardwood floor, slapping the back of his teammates as he went. He had always been an extrovert and was deeply loved and respected by his peers. That night was going to be a very important evening. Don and I had decided to attend a "line" seminar being held at a new local hotel, the Marriott. Our plan was to gather as much information as possible concerning the activities of the distributors during this three-day event. This was not the first time Don and I had worked together in this fashion to gather information. We had visited dozens of homes, rallies and conventions in a blitz of documentation.

Our purpose was to poll as many distributors as we could to determine their "business volume." We would also question the hotel's catering department to find out what the actual costs would be to the promoters of this event. What kinds of profit would be realized from this weekend for those in command? Soon we would have a good idea.

When Don and I arrived at the Marriott Hotel, we could see that the promoters of this event had really gone all out. There was a Rolls Royce parked at the front door. Directly behind it was a 32-foot luxury motor home. We stood together and watched as dozens of Amway distributors took turns sitting in this classic automobile.

"Oh, look at that interiorly exclaimed a young woman, carrying an oversized handbag. She gently and lovingly ran her fingers across the supple leather seats and polished wood trim interior.

"Someday I'm going to own a car just like this!" she declared, now smiling and perching herself into the back seat. The others laughed and crowded around to experience the pleasure of how it felt to sit behind the wheel of this fabulously expensive automobile.

The motor home received the same reverence. There was a line of distributors anxiously waiting, each desiring to see the inside of this luxury coach. Each distributor was easily identified by his large blue "Dream Weekend" nametag. Boy, were they doing just that-dreaming! The retail price on these two vehicles totaled close to a quarter of a million dollars!

Don and I did not waste any time. After watching the distributors with the Rolls and the motor coach, we went about our outlined assignments. We split up and questioned as many of the distributors as possible prior to the evening's program. Our objective was to find out the business volume (approximate amount of retail sales for the month) of each distributor we interviewed.

Approximately 90 percent of all those we interviewed were more than willing to provide us with the much needed information. Our approach was simple and, of course, enthusiastic.

"Hi! My name is Philip Kerns, and I'm doing a story on free enterprise. Would you please assist me in collecting some important information for this vital success story?"

In most cases after securing the name of the distributor, our conversation continued something like this.

"How long have you been in the business?" I asked.

"Oh, I'd say about six months."

"And what was your total business volume this last month?"

"Now wait a minute. That's personal."

"Sure, I understand that, sir, but we're just doing a poll to determine the average business volume of all distributors. This information will be kept confidential." I reassured him.

"I see. Okay. Well, it was $175 this last month."

"Have you ever had a better month?"

"Nope."

"Thanks so much. I appreciate your cooperation!"

Just as soon as I would finish one interview, I'd turn to start another. Sometimes I'd glance at the person I had just talked to, only to see that he was telling others I was doing a story. This would invariably cause some excitement. It wasn't uncommon for a mob of enthusiastic ladies to follow me through the lobby, clawing at me and begging for an interview. It was all in fun, of course.

But I couldn't afford using time for only fun. Too much attention in this posh hotel lobby could cause me to be banished. Some of these meetings were considered "closed functions" because of the type of information given. Only distributors from this line of sponsorship could attend. Whenever this interviewing generated too much activity, I'd politely thank them for their time and slip away to find my partner.

Over a period of several months, we interviewed 156 distributors. We found that the average business volume of the combined group was $402 per month. Strikingly, this figure came close to the one Amway posted in its monthly magazine as required by the FTC. I learned later by studying the final report from the FTC that Amway was ordered to print this information. It was not merely an act of volunteerism.

This polling helped confirm the reliability of the company's statistics. Amway reported that the overall average active distributor produces only $454 in business volume each month. That is a gross earnings before operating expenses of about $135 (based upon a 30 percent margin for retail profit) each month for retail sales. If you wholesale the products, the earnings drop drastically. This is hardly enough money to pay for much in the way of operating costs such as gas, other car expenses, supplies and the like, let alone some of the expensive weekend events one is encouraged to attend. Tickets for these events range anywhere from $4 at the door up to $280.

Finally it was time for the rally to begin. Don and I now stood and watched as hundreds of people stood in line to enter the hotel ballroom. To the rear of this large room, one could see a well dressed tailor measuring a rather large portly man for a suit. He was bending over with his arms expanded from waist to heel, carefully stretching his tape vertically along the trouser leg. I watched carefully as he held this position for quite some time. I could see that he wanted the measurement to be exact.

It was 7:55 p.m. and in just five minutes the doors would open to the ballroom. in order to kill some time and to get a better look at the transaction, I stepped closer to the tailor and his customer. Behind them stood a long rack of handsomely designed three-piece suits.

All of a sudden, a very stylishly dressed brunette came up and took the arm of the tailor's patron. The gentleman seemed quite pleased that she had joined him. I watched carefully as he reached into his jacket and removed his wallet. He carefully counted out several large bills and was promptly given some change and a receipt. The tailor and his client shook hands. The tailor gave a stiff respectful bow, and the customer turned, put an arm around his confrere and walked happily away. Onlookers nodded in approval. It was quite a show.

I thought to myself, "Couldn't he have purchased this same suit for much less at a retail outlet?" Then I remembered my first rally when I had purchased a ring for my wife. I had questioned Lester about the table full of expensive jewels, but he had said that they were being provided by local wholesalers, which he had invited to participate in the rally. However, later when my wife had her ring appraised, we learned I had paid full retail price, plus some.

Clearly, concessions are an important part of these rallies. The magnitude of this unorthodox traffic is enormous, and the cash profits resulting from it are huge.

The doors had now been opened for several minutes. It was a beautiful ballroom with exquisite chandeliers. The tables were adorned with crisp white linen tablecloths, crystal and fine china. The water-filled goblets glistened in the dim light. Scurrying to and fro across the floor were well mannered waiters and busboys attending to the needs of those now seated. Each attendant, properly dressed in a white jacket with gold buttons and shiny black slacks, was ready to assist. Don motioned me to follow him and together we slipped into the kitchen. We found a doorway unattended next to the speakers' platform. This was where we waited and watched. All around us scurried the hotel staff carrying trays of various entrees. They were so busy serving the 1,500 hungry guests that they never even blinked at us.

As soon as the meal was over, the lights were dimmed even more; and once again, as in most such functions, the band began to play. This time a triumphant march set the stage. The announcer named the couple to be honored, and then the spotlight was swung to the side door. just as I had witnessed at dozens of these events, a long procession of distributors filed past the crowd up to the stage. Every achievement was recognized no matter how small.

Now was the moment for which everyone had been waiting. The host was standing at center stage, edifying the individual he was about to present. Sometimes this narration would go on for several minutes, elaborating on how much this person (usually Diamond level or above) loved everyone in the audience and how everyone should listen to each and every word he was going to say if the listener wanted to be successful.

I looked out at the sea of faces. The speaker seemed to hold them spellbound. Some were nodding and smiling approvingly to their neighbors. Others just shook their heads up and down showing their approval to his statements. All appeared to be hanging onto his every word.

As I stood there, I found myself concentrating so hard on these reactions that I missed the big introduction of the honored guest. As I analyzed the individual faces, I was so fully absorbed in their expressions that the throbbing of the band could only be faintly heard in the background. Suddenly I awakened from my trance of thought and turned to the platform. The leader now jerked his coat from his back and threw it over a chair. He stormed back and forth across the stage, exhorting his listeners to be winners, not failures! He bellowed out his message with promises of freedom and financial independence. Frequently, he would pause to absorb the enthusiastic applause of his listeners.

As I watched this exhibition, my sub-consciousness reminded me of the statements I had previously missed:

"Ladies and Gentlemen, the greatest leader who ever lived. Our BODY could not exist without a head like this. The most wonderful man in the world..."

It suddenly hit me that this was how they had announced this leading dignitary! I had heard that sort of glorification at rallies all over the country. "But isn't Christ the head of the church body?" I thought.

The crowd was now laughing. As I looked up, I could see this leader, who was exalted much like a god, moving even faster than before. Body gyrations and descriptive arm and head motions accompanied his every word.

"Do you people out there want to be free?" The crowd now sprang to its feet and screamed back to him, "Yes! Yes!" Their arms were stretched outward and upward, hands open, in a Pentecostal fashion. Many were swaying and waving their arms back and forth as they responded to the speaker.

"How many of you people want to tell the boss to kiss

off?" Again the crowd screamed back, even louder than before. The applause now became rhythmic. They all stood and clapped in unison. Some stamped their feet while others beat on the tables! It just kept going on and on. This pseudo Christ like figure lifted his hands towards the heavens and nodded his head to each beat. It was an orgy of enthusiasm.

Even after the crowd sat back down, their voiced responses continued. Each statement the speaker made generated more excitement in the crowd. The beating of the tables became more intense. Then those sitting at the table closest to me stood again. Hundreds of enthusiastic followers all across the room followed suit. Each was fully engrossed in the leader's words. As I looked out into that sea of faces, every eye appeared to be fixed upon the speaker with a glassy stare. They seemed hypnotized.

One black fellow directly across from me was beating the table so hard with his fist that the water goblets were beginning to spill. His face expressed utter jubilation, and his body was rocking to the throbbing beat.

Hundreds were now screaming at the top of their lungs, encouraging the speaker on. Dozens of individuals stood on their chairs; some whistled while others took their napkins and twirled them over their heads like rodeo stars.

I couldn't believe what I was seeing. It just wouldn't stop! For a moment the noise began to die down, and I thought they were going to quit. Instead the unified clapping took an intense upswing. They were now whistling, stamping and beating on the tables faster than ever. The noise was deafening. Bodies were twisting, jumping and dancing to the beat.

The speaker was dripping with sweat. His head was nodding with intense rhythmical sways. His hands, fists clenched beat up and down as if striking invisible drums. He intermittently lifted his arms upward and outward in a victory like stance.

"What do you need if you're going to succeed?" he roared into the microphone.

The crowd responded instantly. They knew the answer, and without missing a beat they chanted loudly, "Books, tapes, rallies! Books, tapes, rallies! Books, tapes, rallies! Books, tapes, rallies! Books, tapes, rallies!"

After what seemed like an eternity of chanting, the leader, much like the conductor of an orchestra, thrust his hands out slashing the air in an apparent signal for the crowd to stop. Instantly the room became silent. One could have heard a pin drop.

Then, after a few moments, one could see that people were now looking at each other. Some were smiling. Others were laughing. The host for the evening's program was now making announcements of future events, and the black fellow near me, like many others throughout the room, went around and began to shake the hands of everyone within reach.

"Ain't it great? Man, I'm excited!" he would exclaim to each person. Many, in turn, would acknowledge that they, too, were excited.

This fellow then came up to me and put his sweating palm into mine and with a gleaming smile asked, "Are you excited, Brother? Are you excited?"

I really didn't know what to say, so I just returned the smile. He went on and shook another dozen hands, expressing the joy and delight that he felt that night.

This same type of electricity was being generated all over the room. Don came and stood next to my side. I wondered what he was thinking.

All of this allegiance shown to the leader reminded me of what Lee Brown, Diamond Direct, had told a crowd at a different function. He urged them on with words similar to the following:

"Step out on faith now, not understanding, like I did not

understand. I didn't know what it was all about, but I believed in my friend. I believed in my sponsor! And I stepped out in faith, not knowing what to do; but everything he suggested I did. But I also believed my sponsor and my friend would not do anything to hurt me. Do as your friend and your sponsor will do. Accept that on faith. And do that what is suggested for you to do. And just follow these principles which are proven to work, to have whatever you want in life!"

As I reflected on Brown's words, I felt Don nudge me. "C'mon, let's get out of here, Phil. All of this is making me sick. How could we possibly have been taken in by all of this at one time? We were so blind."

I stood fast and took one last long look. I felt compassion. My heart ached for all those I was watching.

"Phil, let's get out of here," Don pleaded. I surrendered to my friend's request. It seemed that reaching those people with the truth would be an insurmountable task, but I knew we had to try.

As Don and I walked back to the car, I remembered another event where the speaker seemed to hold this same kind of mesmerizing power over his fold. It was still vivid in my mind. The crowd really wanted to believe. The room was filled with the same type of hype and electricity.

As I reflected on that other event, I remembered the words, which he so dynamically exclaimed.

"I know what I'm going to have to say when I see someone who's got his nose so high in the clouds that if he walked outside and it was raining, he'd drown to death. I know what I'm going to have to say. I'll just have to say I've got a really good friend. No, this really good friend didn't have status. He got down on his knees and washed people's feet. And you know, baby, he made you and I. His name is Jesus Christ. So what gives you the right to have status?..."

Don was now driving up Powell Boulevard. He pushed

the accelerator to the floor, and I sunk back in the seat, trying to remember more of what this distributor had said and why he had such an apparent hatred for status seekers. What was the real motive for his speech? His later statements revealed more of his intent.

"Now they got some books on the table back there. Be my guest. As a matter of fact, if I was back next to that book table, I'd be throwing them out into the audience because that's what you need. That's where it's at. Read! Read! Read! Listen to tapes!"

I was dead tired, and I fell asleep immediately upon reaching Don's place. I slept until late morning, and when I awoke, I just lay there and thought back upon the events of the preceding night. It had all seemed like a dream—the Rolls Royce, the motor home, the tailor, the ballroom, the speaker, the hype—but I knew full well that it was not. It had really happened.

When Don finally got up, we sat at the table with a cup of coffee and analyzed not only the events of the night before, but all of the functions we had attended that month. This had become a ritual for us. In the past we, too, had been caught up in the put-on glamour and magic of these types of festivities; but now we were looking below the surface.

I would venture to believe that Amway distributors are motivated more than any company in America. Some distributors attend functions every week of the year. There are, for example, "Nuts and Bolts Seminars," "Dream Weekends," "Family Reunions," "Diamond Opens," "Pearl Opens" and a myriad of other sessions which climax with the biggest event of the year, "Free Enterprise Day."

The "Dream Weekend" at the Marriott Hotel proved to be a great financial success, not necessarily for those in attendance but for its sponsor. We learned from the catering department that the actual cost charged by the hotel per person for the program was $54.75. However, the host of the event charged $90 per ticket, thus grossing $135,000. The total gross profit was $52,875, as there were 1,500 in attendance. That's certainly not bad for a weekend's work. Of course, this figure includes only the tickets. It does not include the profits made from the sale of books, tapes, automobiles, programs, clothes and other concessions. That's all additional profit! One distributor told me that most Diamonds put on 10 to 12 rallies per year, and if they are not making $50,000 per weekend on concessions, they are just plain stupid!

Remember the "West Coast Free Enterprise Day" held at the Portland Coliseum? Well, the following year I did some research about that event. The stadium manager told me, "Free Enterprise Day was a mad house! And if you thought that the event you attended was crazy, how about this year. There were 17,000 present."

He went on to explain that it cost $2,000 per day to rent the arena for a total cost of approximately $6,000 for the three-day event. Tickets sold for $18 each so that translates out to $306,000. When you subtract the $6,000 cost, you see a $300,000 gross profit—for ticket sales only. All of the other items that were sold, no doubt, added greatly to the gross profit figure, perhaps even multiplying it several times.

But you say, "Hold it! What about costs like the band who played that famous 'Rocky Theme?'" I spoke with two members of the band, Marvin Bright and Daniel Lents. Both complained that they were never paid to play at these functions. In fact, the host insisted that they pay their own admission fee, transportation and lodging.

He's just greedy," said Lents. "Now that's what I call beating the band!"

We have only touched the surface on possible profits. Let's take a closer look at the kinds of money that could be made from the sale of concessions as well as rally tickets.

The following is an example of total gross receipts which might possibly be made:

17,000/2 (couples) buying 1 tape pack @ $39	$331,500
17,000/2 (couples) buying 1 book @ $5	$ 42,500
17,000 tickets sold @ $18 =	$306,000
Total Gross Receipts	$680,000

I believe I am being conservative in this example because many distributors buy boxes of books (paying full retail price) at these events to sell or distribute to their downlines. it is also considered taboo for distributors to attempt to purchase non-Amway produced books from local wholesalers.

The leaders, therefore, have a captive market—a market that is, in my opinion, incredibly more lucrative than Amway could ever be! Remember, this example is for just one event. Canon, Wells, Hall and others fly to and fro across the country and hold event after event each year.

The number of persons in attendance at this rally. Lester has had over 15,000 present at his Atlanta conventions.

Let's look at another aspect of this non-Amway produced business. If you are subscribing to a "Tape of the Week" Club, which would cost approximately $30 for eight weeks, you would be spending an additional $195 per year for tapes. If only one half of the entire Amway population, or approximately 500,000 distributors, subscribed to this program, that alone would add up to a staggering gross receipts of ninety-seven and one-half million dollars ($97,500,000.00) per year!

I have in my possession a distributor's income chart (non-Amway produced) which purports that the largest amount ever earned by selling AMWAY PRODUCTS in a given year was approximately $416,000. How did John

Wells earn over $70 million in one year as was claimed? Was it on Amway products, or was it on concessions?

Thousands of distributors each year go to functions all over the country as well as abroad. Millions upon millions of dollars are spent at events on non-Amway produced materials, which can be found stacked in heaps and mounds on concession tables everywhere. From my estimation, during fiscal year 1981 Amway distributors may possibly have contributed in excess of $791 million' on concessions to be motivated!

I found a distributor who stated that he spent 56 1/2 cents for every dollar worth of Amway products he bought during a six-month period. I took his number and multiplied it by the retail sales amount of $1.4 billion as reported by Amway Corporation in 1981. I have spoken to distributors who claim this figure (56 1/2 cents) is higher while others say it is lower.

CHAPTER 8

Genuine Treasures

L ife in Lincoln City, Oregon is tranquil in January. One can avoid the hurry and scurry of tourists and traffic, which overwhelms this coastal city during the summer months.

My wife and I have time and time again returned to this little town to enjoy both the solitude of the day and the joy of each other. Some of our friends believe we are "looney" to go strolling hand in hand along the beach during this season of the year. After all, most of the shops are boarded up for the winter, and the weather can be dreadful But it is moments like these that I cherish the most—the times when the weather would become too unbearable and we would laughingly retreat to the nearest cafe, usually overlooking the sea.

God has given me Victoria, such a beautiful gift, and together we are able to simply share one another and marvel at all creation. We have come to the conclusion that we don't really need material success in our lives, at least we do not want to be obsessed with obtaining it. Our lives are flourishing and prospering in many other ways, though not in monetary terms. We have already been married eleven years and our son Timmy, who is a joy to us, has grown up and graduated to soccer, Cub Scouts and basketball.

We don't have much, at least by some people's standards. But we know we have each other and for us, that's what counts!

As my wife and I stood peering into a craft shop window carefully protecting ourselves from the rain, I thought about my nephew Garron, who is blind. He has suffered all his life. As an infant his eyes were removed to prevent the spread of cancer. Now at the age of eight, another medical team is preparing to remove a large tumor from his skull. He is a remarkable pianist; so much so, in fact, that his gift is often shared before audiences in his own hometown.

Garron knows what fate may await him in that operating room, but he has a tremendous source of courage. It comes from heaven above. No material or carnal possessions or human touch could create the strength he possesses. He is not a child who would covet, probably because his blindness protects him from coveting.

One day while I was talking with Garron, he confided in me a secret he had on his heart: "Uncle Phil, there is only one thing that I want in life, and that is to go to heaven and be with Jesus. This life holds nothing for me except pain."

Garron's faith is wonderful, and it has touched the lives of many people. I just wish more people could see that there is more to life than just being mesmerized by money or material things. Certainly it is okay to have possessions. I just don't believe possessions should possess you. To possess material things or money is one thing; to be obsessed by them is quite a different thing. Life is full of riches. Just look about and you'll find them. Look up and you'll find the greatest treasure of all.

CHAPTER 9

The Complaint

It was December 9, 1981, at approximately 5 p.m. when I received a telephone call from Don Griffin. I had previously asked Don to find for me any complaints in the United States addressed to consumer protection agencies which would specifically allege abuses concerning either the sale of concessions or emotional injury to distributors. Up to this time, most of the complaints we were able to compile either referred to products or non-payment difficulties. Don had always been a whiz at research, but I was astounded once again by his ability to retrieve information.

"Phil, I've found what you've been looking for! And more! And it is right hereon the West Coast!" Don stammered. I could tell by his voice that he had discovered something valuable.

"Well, what is it?"

"Now listen carefully. There's this fellow in Portland, Oregon. His name is Bret Sutter. He is a building developer and an Amway distributor. This guy filed an official 29-page complaint to the Amway Corporation purporting mind control by some distributor organizations, and he has documented some of the same things you've seen. I talked to the guy, and the whole thing is really revealing! "How do I get in contact with him?" I asked anxiously.

"He's waiting for your call. Now I'm not sure about this, but I believe he's really frustrated because Amway hasn't done much in response to his complaint."

I called the number Don had given me. I found a somewhat suspicious voice on the other end.

"Hello."

"Bret Sutter?"

"Yes."

"I received a call from Don Griffin with whom you spoke.

Bret interrupted, "Mr. Kerns, can we meet somewhere and talk?" "Of course. Where would be a good rendezvous point?" I asked. We didn't waste any time. I met Bret at the Red Lion Inn within the hour.

Bret's story as I was soon to learn, was spellbinding. I sat across the table from this blonde, thinly framed man and listened intently as he described, in detail, the circumstances leading up to his complaint.

Bret was unique—so different from most of the distributors I had interviewed. He possessed a keen awareness of what was going on. He also was well-schooled and retained a self-possessed ability to communicate his feelings and observations.

"Mr. Kerns, I got into this business solely for the purpose of increasing the bottom line!" "Please, just call me Phil," I interrupted.

"Sure, well, okay Phil. As I was saying. . .

He appeared frustrated that I had broken his train of thought. I felt he needed to get this story out. It must have been building up inside of him. He contemplated his words before speaking.

"I got into this business to make money. Nothing else. As the months went by, l discovered it was much more than that! A lot more was going on. Do you know what a cult is, Phil?"

"Of course," I replied, realizing his question was rather strange. It was as if he were probing to find out whether or not he could trust me with what he wanted to share. I encouraged Bret to continue.

"I believe things have been allowed to get out of hand. It's like a herd of cattle running through Times Square, trampling all over people."

"What makes you so sure?"

"Look I have no quarrel with Amway, okay? Their business concepts are great. It's just that I feel when you've got over one million little toadies running around out there. It's awfully difficult to keep them all in line!" "Okay," I interjected. "But what makes you feel it's a cult or that it may be out of control?"

"First of all, I didn't say the company was a cult! However, I believe some key people on the Amway Distributors' Association Board and thousands of people downline are using the same techniques the cults are using in order to control the minds of the people in their groups. I believe they study this stuff, and they know precisely what they are doing. It's gotten crazy! I'll explain the cult thing a little later, okay?" 'Sure.'

'Now let me go on. You see Amway tells you this is your own business. But in some lines of sponsorship, the leaders do not let you operate it as your own business! You've always got some twerp upstream telling you what to do. When you break off and go' direct' to the company for your products, supplies and other needs, you're supposed to be really independent. Right? No way! They still keep the chain of command strictly intact. Sure, the FTC ruling says they are not a pyramid. Technically speaking, Amway is not a pyramid. Their manual purports they are a direct distributorship business, but behind the scenes, many of these little ole brainwashed toadies are moving millions of dollars worth of non-Amway produced products such as books, cassettes, easels and rally tickets. You name it! These lower echelon distributors and newcomers have absolutely no idea what's going on, not to mention that they never see a dime from this junk. They just flush this stuff downstream, and others eat it up. There is such a large appetite created for this stuff that one can imagine practically no end to the volume they can push.

"Man, they're running around with tapes in their cars, tapes in their homes and tapes at work. Everybody is listening to the 'Dream' and how they are going to get rich. It's the slickest thing happening in America today. Millions and millions of cash receipts are being raked off by a select few from the high-volume peddling of all of these non-Amway produced materials. People are told, and they believe, that they must have them in order to succeed. I am absolutely sick of the whole thing." "Bret, tell me about the cult angle?"

"Okay." Bret sat up straight and continued. "Have you ever heard of Dr. John Clark, Jr., a professor at the Harvard School of Medicine?"

"No, can't say that I have."

"Well, he did an extensive study on all these little toasted groupies as they walked out of the back door of your local guru meetings, and he came up with some pretty interesting thoughts. I found that the points he was making were describing a perfect profile of your class A-1 brainwashed Amway distributor." Bret pulled a large yellow piece of paper from his pocket and began reading its contents.

"They appear to have become rather dull and their style and range of expression is limited and stereotyped. They are animated only when discussing their group and its beliefs. They rapidly lose a knowledge of current events. When stressed even a little, they become defensive and inflexible and retreat into numbing clichés. Their written or spoken expression loses metaphor, irony and the broad use of vocabulary. Their humor is without mirth!"

He also described programmed people and the character-istics of a cult.

I reached over and touched Bret's arm to stop him before he could continue. "Now tell me, where have you seen someone being programmed?"

"That's simple. You're programmed every day—every time you turn on the TV Programming is a gradual sort of thing. Doctors have been saying for years that the human mind is always more susceptible to suggestion whenever there is excitement present."

I began to understand. "So that's what they do-at these meetings?" I thought to myself.

Bret went on: "The band, the bragging, those colorful pictures of Cadillacs, Mercedes and Rolls Royces. It's all part of the plan I And once they get you, they gradually pro-gram you into seeing things their way."

"What about the guys who surround the leader? Aren't they suspicious?" I asked.

Bret began to laugh aloud. "Sure, they know what's going on. But the only thing that the leader cares about is whether or not they are loyal. That's all. The reason I was laughing is because in my complaint to the Amway Corporation I described, in detail, how they break a man and test his loyalty. Now you're going to think this is really bizarre, but," Bret broke out laughing again. "Really, Phil, it's not funny, but... (gulp) but I just can't help myself every time I think about it.

"You see on several occasions I questioned one of my uplines' Dean Robertson, regarding the idea of the leader being the 'God man'—you know, the oracle of God crap? We're told by our uplines to shave and to have that clean look, but what about the leader! He's got twigs sticking out all over his face. But that's okay because he's arrived and he's supposed to be our figurehead.

"Robertson has told me, 'We use the same techniques that the Nazis used. Hitler used it for evil, and we use it for good.'" Bret continued. "All of what Robertson was saying didn't make sense until some of these Diamonds started to publicly humiliate people. Here's exactly what they would do."

Bret leaned across the table and began reading directly from his papers. "I should note at this point that at the Kenney's Family Reunion, Wells held a meeting for those at 1,500 PV (point value). A friend of ours, who subsequently quit the business, attended that meeting. Another distributor and friend who also later quit the business came to us with the following report.

"At the meeting John Wells entered the room with a squirt gun. He mounted the stage and announced that he was going to test the total faith of the Directs. He called all Directs and Silver Producers up on stage and instructed them to strip to the waist. They did so. He then teased them with the squirt gun, ordering some to do a number of push-ups and so forth. Two were ordered to drop their pants, which they reportedly did. One was Marvin Curtiss, and the other was Dean Robertson.

"Kathleen Emery is in possession of the photographs showing Robertson, Curtiss and the others. She volunteered to show the photographs to one witness and did so. The other witness was present at the meeting. A few weeks later Lucy, my wife, was with a couple of individuals who were talking about the incident. They said that distributors are sometimes required to humiliate themselves in public places to show their loyalty to their uplines. Through this process it is known that they can be trusted and can be depended upon to do what they are told."

"Incredible," I thought to myself. "This all sounded so familiar-the hype, the dream goals, the misrepresentation, all of the pressures exerted upon these people, and now this!

Humiliation tactics! Were they actually testing their loyalty?"

"That sounds so much like the tactics of Jim Jones and his inner circle," I thought. I looked and listened to Bret more intensely than before.

Bret continued, "My complaint went before the Amway Distributors' Association Board. Ed Postma, the Sales Coordinator for the Northwestern Regional Sales Department, said that it caused quite a fracas. In fact, I believe my complaint, along with lord knows what other issues, caused the board to reevaluate their position. The reason I believe this is true is because the board, shortly after I filed my complaint, published their manifesto on April 16,1980.

"I believe they were freaking out, especially after that Federal Trade Commission bout. It seems to me that this manifesto is an attempt to correct some of these practices. Allow me to read you Chapter 3 of the manifesto."

Again, Bret read from his documents:

"The only requirement which distributors can impose on prospects whom they are willing to sponsor is that the new distributor shall have an official Amway Sales Kit (without substitution or alteration), sign the SA-88 Distributor Application form and mail it to Amway.

"A new distributor must not be required, as a condition to becoming a distributor, to purchase a specific product volume, maintain a specific minimum level of product inventory, procure a 'starter' or 'decision' pack, purchase tapes, books and other materials or attend meetings, seminars or rallies; however, many of these may be desirable or important to the development of their business."

"Correct me if I'm wrong, but what you are telling me, Bret, is that Amway and the Amway Distributors' Association Board in their manifesto are saying, 'Hey, we don't want you heavy bowlers out there cramming all this unnecessary non-Amway produced paraphernalia down the distributors' throats. Right?"

"Exactly!"

"Is this activity still going on?" I asked.

"You bet it is! I know plenty of people who will tell you that many of these distributors have more non-Amway produced junk in their garages than Amway products."

"Why?" I asked.

"Because they're told that without these valuable tools, they cannot succeed. They'll fail. It's ridiculous. They can't get ahead because they're spending a fortune on this garbage. The tapes and books don't tell you how to build a successful Amway business. They are just full of philosophy and religious wisecracks. They only emphasize how to sponsor new people (which creates new consumers for the non-Amway produced junk). The leader's market is not the general public; it's his own distributor force so retailing is not stressed."

After this engagement with Bret Sutter, I learned that the distributors named in his complaint were required to defend the allegations made against them.

Sutter's complaint cited a myriad of subjects. How ever, two of the key issues were (1) misrepresentation of the sales plan and (2) programming for the sole purpose of having unsuspecting individuals purchase non-Amway produced materials and attend seminars—all of which only enriches the leaders.

Later I obtained letters, which were written by those accused in the Sutter matter. These letters of rebuttal revealed that, in fact, Sutter was telling the truth when he said these people were required to strip in front of the audience. However, the respondent of this complaint alleged that it was all only in fun and pointed out that they were wearing bathing suits under their pants.

Was it really only in fun? Or was it a demonstration for a

predetermined result—a means of mind control? Were they, in fact, wearing suits? Regardless of whether it was only in fun or not, the point seems to have been well made: Do as you are told by your upline, without asking questions.

Today Bret is still running a successful Amway business. He says he is satisfied with Amway's response to his complaint; however, he wishes that more would be done to clean up the business. Bret, like many others with whom I have spoken, just wants to run his business of retailing products, privately, and without all of these additional pressures from upline. Sutter feels that if the Amway Distributors' Association Board can't resolve and police this problem, then who will?

CHAPTER 10

The Truck Driver

Information continued to pour in from various sources. Many had now heard that I was investigating these bizarre allegations. Just what kinds of tactics were being used? The meeting that I was to have with Carl Issenberg of Medford, Oregon, gave me a clearer picture of strategies and techniques used by some of the people in this business. It was as if another light had been switched on revealing more about this ever unfolding story.

As I pulled up in front of Carl's bungalow, I saw a tall, slender man with a pleasant smile step outside, motioning me to come in. Once inside, I settled myself down into a comfortable easy chair while Carl paced back and forth. He had a lot to tell me, and he was anxious to get started.

"Mr. Kerns, these people don't care who they step on as long as they make a buck. It's 'Onward Christian soldiers, marching as to war' First they love you into the business. They entice you to comply and buy. Then if you don't see things their way, they discard you like rubbish, all in the name of Jesus."

"Who would discard you like rubbish?" I shot back.

Carl shrugged, "Well, there are so many people involved. It's really hard to say. I, uh..."

He paused for a moment, searching for the words.

"You see, that's really a hard question to answer. The 'legs of sponsorship,' you know, those businesses that practice this type of baloney most likely span all over the globe. Don't get me wrong. Not everyone in Amway acts in this same fashion. There are a lot of fine, well-run businesses."

"Who's pushing people around like this? Get specific!" I urged.

Carl bent over and shook his head back and forth. I anxiously awaited his reply.

"One of them is Warren Perkins, an Emerald Direct in Washington state. In fact, he is my sponsor. You see, I feel that Warren has used me. That's why I was willing to talk to you. I want others to become aware of some of the tactics being used in this business."

I sat back down and leaned forward, listening more intently than before.

"Now when I got into this business, I intentionally decided to be sponsored by Warren Perkins. You see, I had my pick of distributors because I am an Amway truck driver. I still work for the firm, which has a contract with Amway to deliver products to various households throughout the Northwest. From my ledgers I knew Warren was one of those who was moving the largest volume in my area, so I decided to be sponsored by him. Now I wish I had never made the mistake of joining up with him."

I sensed that Carl's spirits began to spiral down. I knew he had much, much more to share. I listened patiently as he described how Warren got him started into this business. He explained what I had heard so many times before, but this time there was a new twist.

As far as Carl was concerned, Warren was a "high roller" and knew how to move quickly. At Carl's first meeting, Warren gave the presentation and afterwards passed out some non-Amway produced book sand tapes to the group. A teach meeting, there after, he did the same. Carl explained that after he had sponsored a sizeable group, Warren sent him a bill for $225.64, the cost for materials passed out at several meetings.

It was a total shock to me! I didn't expect this bill. It was like a slap in the face. Why hadn't he told me that he was going to charge me for these items!" Carl exclaimed.

Later when Carl went to Warren's home, he carried with him all of the non-Amway produced materials he had collected from his downlines and demanded a refund. Warren interpreted this as quitting altogether.

"No, I'm not quitting the business. I'm just quitting your personal sideline of distributing all this non-Amway produced junk!" Carl had retorted.

Warren reluctantly refunded his money minus a five percent restocking fee, but he didn't stop here. The battle was on! After this incident, Warren went around Carl and began to belittle him in front of those who Carl had sponsored.

"Oh, he's negative! He's going to ruin each and everyone's chance for success! I'm telling you that you need these tools!" Warren would make statements like these each time he met with one of those recruited by Carl.

I could now see as Carl shared his account of this backbiting and disparagement that down inside he was hurting. His eyes became clouded, and I could tell he was really upset.

"This guy would never let up," Carl painfully continued. "He went to my friends and said ... I couldn't believe it when he went to those I care for so much and told them Satan had gotten a hold of me, and that's why I was negative."

I had heard of these same tactics being used before. Many were led to believe that this business was ordained by God and anything contrary to what the leaders say or do was of the devil. Didn't this guy, Warren, have a conscience? Here before me sat the by-product of these questionable tactics. What would cause anyone to say or do such things? My only conclusion was greed—an obsession for money.

I changed the subject, and it wasn't long before we were laughing and carrying on like old friends. Carl was truly a warm human being. it was beyond me how someone could treat a person in this way for the sake of money.

Say, Phil, I sure wish I could show you what all of those Amway distributors look like!" Carl exclaimed. Together we laughed.

Carl explained to me that the large white panel truck he drives is generally fully loaded with boxes of Amway products to be delivered on the route. He went on to tell me how almost every garage where he unloaded Amway products would seem to house almost as many non-Amway produced items. There are books, easels, boards, "decision" packs and all sorts of literature. Some garages are literally full with thousands of dollars worth of this kind of inventory. He had witnessed in excess of $200,000 worth in just one day!

It's just as I had thought. All of this activity was really going on—even as Sutter had said, in spite of the manifesto.

"That's how they make their money, Phil!" Carl explained. "Now you can see why in the beginning Warren sold me 200 percent more of this stuff than soap!"

I thought about all of the questions Carl still had not answered. How much more did he know about the business? Could he confirm any of the allegations made in the complaint by Sutter?

I soon found Bret Sutter was not the only one who knew of humiliating incidents such as people removing their pants on stage before an audience. Carl shared how Diamond Direct Fred Doan bragged about taking down his pants for John Wells at a function held back east. He said that this was his way of demonstrating his loyalty to John, and by doing this he knew John wouldn't do anything to hurt him.

"Tell me, Carl, how can you be sure they are really looking for total obedience?" I asked.

Carl turned his head and grinned. "Let me give you an example, he said. "I remember hearing about Fred Locke standing up in front of a crowd and saying, 'The degree of obedience required in this business is if your upline tells you to jump off a bridge, don't ask questions. Do it!"

"How screwy and unbalanced. What did taking down one's pants or jumping off a bridge have to do with selling soap?" I thought to myself.

Carl had seen and heard a lot. He continued. "Phil, have you ever wondered what happens to some of the money that is collected at various functions? I have seen distributors who were hosting events walk up to the money box, and when they thought no one was looking, they would slip some of the cash in to a coat pocket and walk out. The only other person who knew what was going on was the one watching the box. Who is accountable? So many of the functions require only cash, and seldom are receipts given."

The questions that Carl was asking brought to mind a conversation I had with Al Inder, a Pearl Direct from Tacoma, Washington, who said that he was tired of apologizing for an hour and a half for the mistakes of others in this business. Mr. Inder is an Amway veteran, who has been in the business for twelve years, and is one of the 6,000 voting members of the Amway Distributors' Association. He also feels that there is a real possibility that much of the money received from these non-Amway produced materials is not declared as income.

His statements made me wonder how many millions of dollars in cash receipts are escaping the tax bite of the Internal Revenue Service? Does the IRS know that there is a massive "ghost", system of non-Amway produced materials being sold behind the front of this legitimate Amway enterprise? Apparently from what I have learned, this business is widespread. Since talking with Mr. Inder, I have questioned many distributors about the size of this side business, and some have expressed a belief that it is larger than the Amway business itself!

Could that be possible? Bret Sutter in his complaint said that he was spending 56 1/2 cents for non-Amway products versus every dollar he spent on Amway products.

During the course of the time that I talked with Carl, incident after incident kept unfolding, each one giving me additional insight into this business. One particular story that really stands out in my mind was the time Carl met Tom Kenney. He had just gone to a rally at the Marriott Hotel in Portland, Oregon.

"Come on, Carl," Warren insisted. "This is your big chance to meet a Diamond. We'll go up to his suite."

By this time, Carl was already becoming disillusioned with all of the fanfare, but he reluctantly followed Warren upstairs. Both men and their wives had to fight their way down the hallway through the mobs of people to get to Tom's suite.

As Carl walked in along with Warren, he saw the room surrounded with familiar faces including Dick and Kathleen Emery, Steve and Teresa Ferrera and Jim Mate. Directly across the room sat Tom Kenney in his shirt sleeves, wearing a big smile on his face. They all just quietly sat and looked at him.

"Is this a set up?" Carl thought to himself.

Warren moved across the room and pulled up a chair for Carl.

"Carl, this is your golden opportunity. it may be the only one you'll get. If you have any questions that you want to ask Tom, go right ahead."

Carl really didn't have much to say, but he was startled when Tom leaned forward and said, "How would you like to try on my Rolex? Here, go right ahead."

Carl said that he couldn't believe it. This guy was taking off his watch and wanting him to try it on.

'Look, Carl, you don't have to sit there in awe. I'm not god. I'm just a man!"

Everyone in the room laughed in unison except Carl. Carl slipped the expensive watch on his arm, as requested.

"Here, go on. Try on my diamond ring. And if you would like, try on this gold bracelet, too. Someday you just might have one."

Carl told me that he resented this child's play. "Why is this guy trying to dangle 'carrots' in front of my nose?" he thought.

By now everyone in the room was passing around all of Kenney's treasures. Carl carefully concealed his feelings as he bid all good night. When he opened the hallway door, he was met with hundreds of mesmerized admirers, attempting to catch a glimpse of Tom Kenney. Carl violently lunged forward into the crowd, pushing his way to wards the stair well. Carl wanted out. Not only did he want out of this crowd, he wanted out of this kind of business. This obsession with material things was not for him.

A similar episode that Carl related was from a tape he had listened to where John Wellstook Leeand Bobby Jane Brown, now Diamond Directs, out to his luxury motor home. On the counter John had a cardboard box full of cash for them to see. "You can touch it. Go ahead!" he had urged them. As the tape revealed, Lee ran his fingers through the cash.

"This was the same kind of technique used by Lester to entice me into the business," I reflected.

Today Carl Issenberg is out of this "side" business. He no longer is associated with these people. He has built his Amway business independent of all this razzle dazzle and hype. The last time I spoke with Carl, he had approximately

60 downline distributors in his organization and a $5,500 per month business volume. Carl's business is growing. Carl just got new friends.

CHAPTER 11

The Odds For Success

Your income can match your dreams!" This statement
is frequently used by the Amway Corporation and
Amway distributors throughout the world. Can one really
earn large profits and purchase the luxury items that are dis-
played in Amway's literature such as yachts, expensive
automobiles and extended vacations?

Before I answer this question, let's just find out what it is
like to dream. One leader who has thousands upon thousands of distributors in his organization can show us how.
He will be explaining in great detail how to escape the New
England snow.

Can you picture us now? Relaxing and tomorrow the
snow is still four feet high and so we go out to the local air
port to get on a private jet. We walk up the steps that's got
red carpet down the stairway. It says, "Welcome Aboard"
and it's got your name on it. You walk into the private Lear
jet and you turn to the pilot. "Is everything ready?" "Yep."

You and all the kids get aboard. "Let's go to Florida.
Take off for Florida."

Two hours from now you are landing at Miami International Airport. You step down out of the plane. Maybe you had a little snack aboard because your pilots know what you like to eat. You walk out of the plane and up pulls a big black Cadillac limousine. The chauffeur gets out, opens the doors and says, "Step in Mr. and Mrs. John Doe."

You get in. He drives you over maybe to the local yacht club. You walk aboard your private yacht. Maybe it's a hundred feet long, crew of eight, red carpeting coming in. They pull up the gang plank, start the engines, and you take off. And you're cutting through those waves, and maybe those waves are a foot or two high, and you are just breaking the waves. And now it's 90 degrees. The sun's beating down. You go up to the upper deck, and you put your bathing suit on. You lay up there, and you are relaxing. You just feel those little bits of perspiration. Those large drops of water are all over your body. They just start to form from that sun which is drawing the water out of your system.

And you just feel our body's getting a little bit red here and there from the beautiful sun, and a beautiful breeze is coming across. You can feel the body heat, but the breeze is there to make it so cool. Where shall we go? Oh, just take a cruise out aways. Relax. Maybe you lay there for awhile and then your wife says, "Honey the chef has got dinner prepared." So you walk down the circular stairs, walking in your swimsuit into the main dining room which is very elegant. They're all dressed up with their white uniforms with all the gold braid and everything on them cause they got jobs!

The chef says, "I cooked your favorite," and he names this big fancy meal.

And your wife says, "Great."

And you say, "Make me a hamburger."

You sit there and eat and relax. Maybe you go up to the front of the yacht. You put your hand out there and feel the water just breezing by. You feel a little ocean spray. And it just feels so refreshing. You might just take your finger and taste the salt water.

Maybe you sit up there with your wife and put your arm around her. You look over in her eyes and say, "Darlin', I love you. Do you believe this is happening to us? You and I? Remember back home? Probably five feet of snow now. It's hard to believe. Just three years ago we were broke. Remember that rotted out old car we had? You were afraid to wash it because you might find out there wasn't a body under the dirt and the rust? But now here we are... Remember how our friends laughed at us? They said, 'You're going to sell soap? You're going to be in Amway? Oh, those poor people.'"

Sometimes this type of story would go on and on. Evidently, many people in the business believe it is possible to achieve this level of success. As one can see, this person is very successful in painting a fantasy in the minds of his followers. But now let's come back to reality is it really possible for one to achieve this much success in this business?

I remember talking to a young boy at a seminar. He was telling me that someday his parents were going to be "millionaires."

Let's pretend that Amway decided to be benevolent about this whole thing, and they attempted to fulfill everyone's "new found dream" of becoming a millionaire. We know that the corporation reports retail sales in excess of $1.4 billion in 1981. This information is from the 1981 Amway Annual Report, which includes all subsidiaries and affiliates. Obviously, there are substantial expenses, including cost of merchandise, operating expenses and taxes. The net profit would probably be only as mall fraction of the $1.4 billion. We cannot use the actual net profit figure for 1981 because those figures are not available. Interestingly enough the 1981 Amway Annual Report has a very limited amount of financial information. It contains no financial statements or accountants' reports.

For the sake of discussion and in an effort to give the corporation the benefit of the doubt, let's presume the net profit after expenses and taxes equaled 25 percent of the gross retail sales, or approximately $350 million. We also know there were one million distributors according to their manual in this same year. Therefore, the company, if it retained no profits whatsoever, could create only 350 millionaires. But what about the other poor individuals? You know, the other 999,650 distributors? Don't they receive anything for their efforts?

Let's say that the company exclaimed, "Oops, we've made a big mistake! We're going to have to be more democratic about this. In order to fulfill the dreams of a greater portion of the distributors' force, we'll just create 'thousandaires!' Simple as that!"

Now if we have 10,000 distributors earning $35,000 per year that would equal the $350 million. There would still be the corporation and the other 990,000 distributors left penniless. By itself, it's a great deal of money, but $350 million is not very much money when you are dividing it up among a large corporation as well as one million distributors. So, if the average active distributor only sells $454 per month in business volume, who then is making the larger profits?

The illustrations just cited were used only to make a point. However, let's be realistic concerning this issue. In the April 1982 issue of Reader's Digest, it stated that approximately 275 individuals in Amway earned in excess of $100,000 and that only 11 earned in excess of $200,000. We really are talking about a very small number of people in the distributors' organization earning the big money.

Mr. and Mrs. Ken Johnson of Norfolk, Virginia, at one time were Amway Diamond Directs. They verified that there were approximately 6O Diamonds in Amway in 1970. They sold their business in the early 1970's in order to build their own direct distributor business, which proudly claims to pay larger profits than Amway. During an interview Mrs. Johnson told me, "We pay six times as much as Amway on one-fourth of the volume." She also pointed out the reason she and her husband left Amway was because there just wasn't enough money in the business for the field people. "We didn't feel it was fair to keep telling everyone they could make it. Besides, the Amway name, as far as we were concerned, was well overworked."

Using the ratio that the Johnsons gave me, I calculated that there should be approximately 450 Diamonds in Amway today. Gary Hardy, a Diamond from Bellevue, Washington, told me in a phone conversation that there are approximately 400 in the Diamond level and above today. Let's give Amway the benefit of the doubt and say there are a thousand Diamonds. That's still a very small percentage above Direct Distributor.

Amway had been contacted concerning the approximate number of distributors at the various levels. They said that they were unable to give us this kind of information. When one considers that there is a total of one million distributors, what are one's chances of becoming a Diamond? I don't want to say "slim" because that would not be fair. Some just do make it!

Maybe a person doesn't want to be a Diamond I How about one just becoming a Direct Distributor? The only information Amway would disclose concerning levels of achievement was that there were approximately 24,000 persons in 1981 at the level of Direct Distributor or higher. There is sporadic information on levels of achievement published but nothing in its entirety.

Did you know that a Direct Distributor when he achieves the 7,500 point level earns approximately $1,000 per month before paying expenses? In order to achieve this income, the Direct and his downlines have to move approximately $13,000 worth of products each month. How many people does he need in his organization? Well, if one is using Amway's $454 average business volume per distributor, a person would need approximately 30 people in his organization. That may not sound like many, but remember, every single one of these downlines would have to be moving over $400 B.V (business volume) per month. In addition to this, the FTC report said that the annual turnover rate for the average distributor is 50 percent per year. Is someone telling people this business is easy? It's a tough row to hoe!

All of these figures remind me of a story my banker related. She was very close to a couple named Terry and Mark, who lived in Oregon and had just started in Amway. Terry was due to give birth to a child during the same week a rally was scheduled in Spokane, Washington. She had told everyone she was going, due date or not. Her husband said he would attend the rally even if she were in the hospital. Her mother tried to discourage Terry from making the four-hour trip. "What would you do if you went into labor?" her mother asked. Undoubtedly, her mother was totally heartbroken, but she sighed.

In relief when her daughter finally gave birth to the baby a week before the event. That didn't stop this highly motivated couple. They went to the rally anyway and took along their week old infant.

Mark was so confident that he quit his job in order to pursue his Amway "Dream." Shortly after he had left his relatively high paying position, he discovered that he was unable to support his family. The Amway business did not create the profits he had expected. This young family had to start all over again, greatly disillusioned.

Before one accepts and believes any dream, he should ask a few questions first. How much is the dream going to cost? What are the chances of making the dream a reality? What are the "odds for success?" Then get specific answers!

CHAPTER 12

The Broad Way, the Narrow Way and Now Amway

Why was Lester Canon so anxious for me to break Direct and speak before his Atlanta convention? That question always seemed to perplex me so one day I called my previous upline, Mark Hall, to find out the answer.

"Hello, Mark, how have you been?"

"Couldn't be better, Phil I In fact, the wife and I are making plans to move into our new home. It has over 10,000 square feet, five fireplaces and seven bathrooms!"

Mark sounded just as positive and enthusiastic as always, but I didn't want to waste time on small talk so I came right to the point.

Tell me, Mark, why was it so important for me of all people to beat the Canon convention? He usually only invites key people, such as politicians, movie stars and the like."

I could hear Mark chuckling in the background. He always had a great sense of humor, but I noticed that his laugh was not hearty. It rapidly diminished. He knew I needed an answer.

"Are you sure you want to know?"

"Of course, I do."

I waited for a few moments. It sounded as if he were collecting his thoughts.

"Well, it's like this, Phil. Lester can buy literally anything he wants in life-no matter what the price is. He can buy a bank or a hotel or just travel if he pleases. You see, money does not totally gratify him anymore. He's got this giant ego that has to be fed. That's why he likes to stand up in front of all these crowds. It makes him feel really good.

"You were supposed to be part of his ego trip. He wanted to stand up in front of that crowd in Atlanta, Georgia, to show each and everyone that in his downline was an ex-cultist from the People's Temple who had succeeded in becoming a Direct Distributor. He knew, with out a doubt that the people would just eat it up! It would send a reassuring signal to the entire crowd. 'See, if he can do it, you can do it!' It would build and reinforce each person's belief in the business!"

Mark's statement did not come as a total surprise. Somehow I knew all along that this might be a possibility. However, it was likely that Lester was more interested in increasing their belief than in gratifying his own ego. Even though I had divorced myself from this organization, I have not been able to totally relinquish all thoughts concerning the people I have met within its ranks. Most of them are sincere and genuine individuals. Each one is uniquely independent and most likely perceives this business just as it is often portrayed—all American, God fearing and, of course, the best opportunity in the world!

These thoughts lead me to ask the following questions: If some of the leaders of this organization are really all American and God fearing, why do they take advantage of so many of their friends? If they care about others, why would they charge them $280 per ticket to get into a rally and $75 for a set of tapes, and then stand there and tell these same individuals that someday they will achieve the kind of financial success that the leaders have obtained?

If a person loves others, does he go and tell them they're a "loser" because they decide not to continue in his footsteps? If one loves others, does he lie to them about the business and his income by buying possessions he cannot afford, only to entice them?

It seems to me, by the statements they have made, that many of the leaders who have been portrayed in this book really don't love people as they say; instead, they love themselves, and they love money. They are obsessed with money and what it can buy.

But what about all the little guys who are not making any money to speak of? I am reminded of a distributor whom I recently called. I found her name listed in the yellow pages of a telephone book. During our conversation 1 brought up the subject of money. After all, isn't that the reason why we operate a business—to make money? When I asked her what her business volume was, she became defensive. Many do. When I asked if she had made Direct, she angrily replied, "No, but I've been in this business eighteen years. Even if I never make a dime, I'd stay in because of all the loving people."

Another person I encountered lives in Pendleton, Oregon. Prior to quitting, Charles Bartholomew also filed a complaint to Amway Corporation. Interestingly enough, he, too, was sponsored by Warren Perkins, Emerald Direct.

Charles went through the same rude awakening that Carl Issenberg had experienced. Warren went around Bartholomew and bad mouthed him to his downlines because he would not purchase non-Amway produced materials nor attend rallies.

"But how do some of these people afford to go to all of those rallies!" Charles exclaimed. "I went to one rally in Georgia which cost me over $200 for the weekend plus air fare just to hear John Wells' layman Christianity. To top that, when I got there, my room had been changed to a different motel seven miles away from the convention, and I had no car to use."

Warren insisted that Charles attend all functions even if he had to lie to his employer in order to go. "I just couldn't do it. I wouldn't feel right about calling in sick," Charles explained.

Charles told me that God was first in his life and as far as he was concerned, many of the individuals in Amway were turning it in to a religion. Many of the followers were now looking up to the leaders as if they were gods. "I had to get out," he said, "even though I had built a successful business and established my own warehouse to service my down-times. Warren had ruined my business. He had now taken over and was selling all of the products to my people. I had thousands of dollars worth of inventory which I could not move.

"You know, Phil, something else really bothers me, too. Have you ever heard the expression, 'Fake it till you make it ...?'"

"Sure!" I replied and then went on to tell him that this phrase also happened to be the title of the book I was writing.

"Well, as long as I have been in Amway, it's been a very common cliché. Some good friends of mine believed it was such an important aspect of the business that they went out and bought a brand new Cadillac. Financially they were not prepared for it, and it almost forced them into bankruptcy. I have met a lot of people in this business who find 'faking it' to be a justifiable means of building their organization even if they are broke! It is sad to think that they must lie to others, and perhaps even to themselves, about their income in order to look like they are really 'making it.'"

With over 2,000 direct sales businesses in the United

States, why do so many flock to this particular organization? It couldn't be the money because a very small percentage of people make large amounts of money in this business. This is substantiated in the FTC report, which stated that only one-half of one percent of the 340,000 distributors in 1974 earned $10,000 or above.

We II then, if it isn't the money, what is it? I n a nutshell I believe it is this: IT'S THE DREAM—THE PROMISE OF BIG MONEY!

That's all. All those glamorous mental and paper pictures of wealth are still just pictures of wealth. The leaders know people are scratching. People are trying to find their niche in life. They know that they all have hopes! They know that they all have dreams! Can money really fulfill their hopes and dreams? Can it bring contentment and happiness? As I have indicated before, there is a vast difference between the possession of money and the obsession of money.

Solomon is thought to have been one of the wealthiest men in the world or possibly "the wealthiest." In the Bible he admitted, "Pleasure, what does it accomplish?" [Ecclesiastes 2:2, NASB]

He went on to say, "Whoever loves money never has money enough; whoever loves wealth is never satisfied with his income. This, too, is vanity." [Ecclesiastes 5:10, NIV with a dash of KJV at the end]

Solomon confessed in the "Book of Ecclesiastes" that even with all his wealth and greatness, a day would come when he would pass from this world just like the poor man and stand before God in judgment.

Conclusively, he summed up the pursuit of riches as "futility." I agree that this life is a dead-end street unless one has a dream, but that dream will be totally futile if it is an obsession to obtain great wealth.

When I was married but a few months, I witnessed tragedy. A five-year-old boy was crushed under the wheels of an automobile. As I held him in my arms, I became helplessly horrified as the warm blood drained from his body. I remember just sitting there and trembling as I felt him breathe his last breath.

Looking up, I could see a crowd gathering about me. Several people had to restrain the dead boy's mother as she wailed in agony. At the age of 18 it was my first lesson on eternity. The Bible says, "It is appointed that every man will die once." [Hebrew 9:27, RSV] No one shall escape it. Why then is it that so many people feel they must heap up treasures here on earth in order to provide themselves with security when we know it is impossible to take these things with us after death?

Andrew Bates, an Assembly of God pastor, told me, "I wish people in our church had the same zeal for Christ and lost souls as they do for this business. Many times I have gone to the homes of my parishioners who are in Amway, and I have found pictures of Rolls Royces and Cadillacs taped on their refrigerators."

I have found many pastors around the country that feel this very same way. Some individuals would never walk across the street to minister the gospel or assist their neighbor; yet they would drive many hours to share the Amway "opportunity."

Somehow thousands have been led to believe that this is a wonderful Christian organization and that God has put his blessing upon it. So much so that recently Christian magazines have featured articles praising the World of Amway. One Christian editor openly admitted that he knew very little about Amway but printed the article any way. Charles Paul Conn, the author of The Winner's Circle, stated in his book that Amway was not a Christian organization. Yet I have seen function after function being held on Sunday mornings in conjunction with a church service.

Amway Corporation says that it is not a Christian organization. Why then do we constantly hear references to Christianity throughout this vast business? Are the leaders within the distributors' ranks concerned about how the public might possibly view this organization?

Parade printed, in January 17,1982, a Gallup poll listing 24 professions and occupations. They asked 1,564 persons how they would rate the honesty and ethical standards of people in these different fields. Clergymen ranked first in the poll, and car salesmen were on the bottom of the list.

Is it possible that some distributors in the Amway business are putting up a Christian front in order to give their business practices credibility? Why is it that Amway brings up in their compendium this bizarre question: " Is Amway a religious or political cult?" Of course, the corporation denied the question, but why even bring it up? I will let each make up his own mind as to the answers to these questions.

I have written this book from my heart. I cannot be ashamed of the gospel; nor can I, in good conscience, allow millions to be deceived by practices, which make constant misrepresentations of scripture.

Are there "winners" and "losers" in life? Oh sure, there are. But whether one is a winner or a loser is not dependent on whether one is or is not in Amway. There is only one time when a man succeeds or loses in life—when he either makes a decision to follow God or to reject Him. The choice is for each person to freely make. To succeed is to trust God with one's entire life, even when things look futile. To lose is to walk away from the only hope for this world.

Afterword

Not everyone within Amway's ranks conducts business as depicted in this book. Certainly many individuals desire to operate their private enterprises in a conscientious and ethical fashion.

Does Amway realize there is a problem inside the distributors' ranks? Apparently so. The April 1982 issue of Amagram indicates the founders, Jay Van Andel and Rich DeVos, are aware of these internal problems and have addressed this fanaticism in this edition of the magazine.

I contacted Amway's Legal Department in March of 1982, just thirty days prior to this Amway publication and interviewed the Chief Legal Counsel. He sent to me an eleven-page document, which seemed to avoid most of my original questions.

I also asked one of Amway's Legal Counselors how many people had been dismissed for misconduct since the new manifesto had been drafted. His reply was, "Oh, I guess about 10, but not more than 50."

Some of my sources tell me that possibly as many as 200,000 to 500,000 distributors may be involved in deceptive behavior. One person said, "This particular group of distributors always works on the edge of the law."

This same source allowed me to listen to a taped message recently delivered by a Diamond Direct. He instructed the crowd, "We don't lie; we just tell the truth in advance." My point is this: If the Federal Trade Commission can't get a handle on this due to budgetary problems and if Amway's owners won't stop it, then who will?

I hope you will. It is for this reason that the book was written.

Since the book's completion, numerous things have been taking place in the World of Amway. I'll sum them up quickly.

On April 16,1982, the Wall Street Journal reported, "AMWAY DISTRIBUTORS' BIG TAX BREAKS STIR INVESTIGATIONS BY CONGRESS, IRS. "This investigation was headed by Representative Pete Stark of California. Allegations were that distributors were using all sorts of innovative tax deductions as instructed by an ex-IRS agent. The IRS said the ex-agent was "out of line" and that the deductions claimed by distributors were "game playing."

Two weeks later this investigation died. I have sent telegrams to Representative Stark asking him why he backed off from this investigation. I have called his office, but he never returned my calls.

On July 28,1982, the Attorney General of the State of Wisconsin announced that the Justice Department has filed a lawsuit against the Amway Corporation and some of its distributors for misrepresentation of income. He points out in his suit that distributors misrepresent individual or personal incomes utilizing unrealistic, hypothetical or projected income.

Prior to this lawsuit Amway and its distributors were given a Cease and Desist, Order from the Federal Trade Commission. The order insisted that persons in Amway stop misrepresenting income.

The Wisconsin lawsuit bases its allegations upon an income tax audit, which averages distributors' income.

Should the State of Wisconsin be successful in obtaining a judgment, it will be interesting to see what action, if any, the Federal Trade Commission will take.

Printed in the United States
16224LVS00002B/286